Yaqui Woman and the Crystal Cactus

Spiritual Odyssey of a Woman of Power

By

Ric V. Solano

Strategic Book Group

Strategic Book Group
P.O. Box 333
Durham CT 06422

www.StrategicBookClub.com

ISBN: 978-1-60911-622-4

For Teresa, mother; Luz, my mentor;

Zoe, mother of my sons; and

Rosemary, my partner, who closes the circle of loving.

And for women of power everywhere.

Artwork by Lucy S. Mulcahy

Dear Reader: I am a licensed PhD psychotherapist, with years of experience serving people in all walks of life on all manner of mental and family problems. I consider myself a rational, pragmatic professional.

So it was a major surprise to undergo a phenomenal, out-of-body experience that emerged inexplicably without connection to any other part of my life.

On successive nights, I found myself witnessing a series of events ultimately involving a woman named Teresa, said to be a Woman of Power in the World.

Terrifying events involving her life and that of her family emerged. The following is her story and that of her family as I came to observe it. First, however, are words of my own.

1

The Therapist

Truth be told, I am rational and thoroughly realistic in my view of the world and the people in it. But I admit to sometimes believing more than what I see, hear, feel, taste, and smell around me. Maybe my openness comes from lifelong curiosity, sound professional training, interning, and long practice of working with people. Ultimately it has prepared me for admitting to more than what is called *real*.

Eureka! It would be surprising if extensive structured learning and years of experience of working with people were prerequisites to accepting the supernatural or paranormal. As some physicists believe and tell us, we live in a dual universe. Some believe there are simply more dimensions than those we know about and live by. Personally, I think all we need to know about the merits of this theory is to dream. Even though at heart I insist on the scientific method, I am unsure as to what is real. I am in a dilemma!

Still, whatever the ultimate truth is—if there is one—I do not believe I was chosen to observe Teresa and the tragedy that came to her family because of my predisposition. I had not undergone sensory or sleep deprivation, confinement, or extreme exhaustion. Nor had I used hallucinogenic drugs to have the phenomenal experience. I was not seeking to escape from reality.

Likely the dreams happened when in hypnagogic states that occur between sleeping and waking. At first, I saw long visions of Teresa, the woman of power, which lasted through the night. I had previously seen the family's journey of escape that included the rape of Teresa's mother, Maria, and her subsequent nightmares. Then I caught glimpses of further journeys that included more deaths. Ultimately, I witnessed the miraculous birth of Teresa.

Teresa's orphan life began in a church workhouse and continued until her early marriage. After a vision, she pledged as a woman of Seataka, a woman of power. Thereafter came immigrant life and service to women and families in a railroad work camp in Chicago. Here she raised her family, including a daughter, Luz, and ultimately lost her beloved husband. Finally, Teresa died in splendor in rural Arizona in the company of a war-wounded son. Throughout, Teresa, born following a horrific rape, served as a loving, caring woman of power with all persons she encountered. They never forgot her.

Throughout, I observed through the dreams, heard the voices and words, and witnessed the events experienced by the figures involved. At times I also experienced the thoughts and feelings of the people I observed and viewed events through their eyes.

In retrospect, I believe my selection as the dream observer was arbitrary, except that I was accepting of the phenomenal experience. It is clear, however, that someone was needed to narrate the tragedy that befell the Yaqui people and this family so that what happened would not remain unknown. The presence of this unique, powerful woman in our universe should also not go unrecognized.

Ultimately, too, the dreams contained a powerful message. The message reminds us of an ongoing truth—that our world contains women of goodness and power who help us to love and to build better lives.

2

Teresa

My name is Teresa. I am old now, and finally I have chosen to live with Juan, a son I love very much. There is much to tell before I die, and I want to share what happened to me in my long life. Forgive my way of saying things; I will try to be clear in what I say.

I was told much of this story by my grandmother who was really not my grandmother but a lovely woman who cared for me. She was old, the housekeeper of the priest who also cared for me. She told me that my life began with hurt. I shall tell more of that later. For now, I want to speak of a miracle that few people experience: as a young woman and a new wife, I had a vision.

In the vision, I was told that in my time I would come to know of people's suffering. There would be people, the vision said, who would live with greed and violence and make harmful choices that would seem natural to them. Few people would care for others, especially for those who were hurting. Then, too, said the vision, there would be a few special women who would come to protect those who could not care for themselves. Those few would help uncaring people see their own beauty. Their lives would be an example of how to be in the world.

I confess that I did not always believe that there were special people present in the world. I felt that people were only hurtful toward others and would remain so. After my vision, I was still unsure.

Had I but believed, I would have known that the vision was real and that I would live it. I would not have needed proof of goodness in the nature and spirit of things. I lived with the vision for many years but somehow overlooked its lesson. Perhaps I needed time, perhaps watching my children grow up, perhaps losing my dear partner, Francisco. Eventually I knew I needed to return to what I had first learned. That need led me back to San Ignacio, a village in Baja California, Mexico, and to a mountain standing at the foot of its ancient cemetery.

3

Returning

I, the observer, heard the foregoing words spoken that I learned later were Teresa's as an older woman. It was the night of the first dream and the beginning of my out-of-body experience. Teresa was speaking of her need to return to a vision she had first experienced as a new bride. There were other bits of information, too.

A very young Teresa and her husband Francisco were eager to start a new life in Chicago, having just gotten married in Mexico. Because he was from a wealthy family and older than Teresa, Francisco had possessions that he was able to sell to enable them to leave directly. However, on the night before their departure Teresa had a mysterious dream. Here I interpret her words:

I told Francisco of it and that the dream would not leave me. The dream instructed me to go to San Ignacio, a place neither of us had heard of nor had our friends. We later learned it was in Baja California, Mexico. Francisco said he would not go, wherever it was. It was out of our way, he said, and it would be an added cost. This was our first argument.

At last I found a traveling merchant in Leon who told me where San Ignacio was and how to get there. After more arguments, I convinced Francisco to go, and we left for that village. I was especially excited about my dream. Francisco was less convinced of what I would learn in San Ignacio than I was. But finally he was willing to go.

We made the long, hot journey by farm wagon, railroad car, and even by horse, and we finally arrived at San Ignacio. During the journey,

Francisco asked repeatedly about the dream, what it was about or what it meant. I remember him saying, "I'm not believing that you know nothing of what the dream meant or what you'll be looking for, or even what that dream is about. Or maybe you just don't want to tell me!" Maybe it was the heat or his tiredness, but Francisco grew angry or just withdrew. I was patient with his many questions, and what I told him was true—that I did not know anything more than I had told him but only that the dream held a vision.

We arrived still feeling strong love for each other, even though we had argued. That afternoon we found a small house with rooms to rent run by a gentle woman who also provided meals. I asked about a store that sold books because Francisco liked to read and I didn't want to tire him if I had to wait to be called as it said I would in my vision. Fortunately, there was a stationery-bookstore nearby that Francisco could visit while I waited.

The next day after breakfast, I waited, half sleeping and lying down. Towards evening, I began to feel a strange sense of time. Shortly I thought that the feeling had gone away. However, when Francisco returned I was lying upon our bed in what he thought was a deep sleep. Later, he told me he left quietly leaving the door open, expecting me to rouse and call him. That night I never awakened from my dream.

At daybreak I awoke to find Francisco sitting outside the doorway where he had slept. All was silent and still as I left him. Time felt strange, and all seemed distant, even separate from me. I seemed to pause, stop, and observe Francisco anew. I described the world with words I had not even known before. I left the rooming house early that morning and was gone into late afternoon.

When I returned to our room, Francisco was stretched out on our bed, unmoving, wearing the same peaceful look I had seen on his face before leaving that morning. As he had said earlier, he was exhausted from the trip. But he was as loving as before.

Later over supper, I thought of how to describe what I experienced that day. I tried, but even my new words did not capture what had come to me. Words seemed uneven, shallow, almost meaningless as if they were standing for something else but were failing to convince.

Then the account of what I had seen and heard emerged uneven and broken up. I began saying, "I heard and saw so much. It was beautiful, and I know it is not clear. Still, it was happening before my eyes like a fairytale." Francisco had cold disbelief showing in his face, and I knew that none of what I tried to say made sense. He never doubted my experience, but he just could not believe it.

But all that had happened in the past. Many human years later, I feared having lost the message of that first vision. And I never forgot the yearning to return and the need first felt to go to San Ignacio, however. I knew I had to return to that place of the vision.

So years later as an old woman, I decided to go back and relearn what I had forgotten.

I feel old, perhaps tired, but old in many other ways. I move slowly and think about at things I remember with more care. Maybe that is why I needed to come back to that important moment in earlier life, to understand it better and to learn. The moment was so mysterious that maybe its mystery led me to put it aside. Maybe I thought that it could not be real. And yet, somehow, I believed it. I needed to know more of it, to understand it better. So this time, now that my beloved Francisco is dead, I asked my son Juan to accompany me to San Ignacio. He came like his father, complaining a little, though less so. He is as patient as his father.

I sit alone in a small, quiet room of almost the same rooming house where Francisco and I stayed many years ago, back when I was such a young girl. Back then I was called to a dream early in a dark morning, called to begin a climb of a small mountain that lay beyond the house and a small cemetery.

And now, these many years later, I have again been waiting. The call to return to the mountain comes in a sound that grows softly like the awakening shudder of one of my children. It simply begins. I had begun to doze as if preparing for the dream. Now in those early moments, I hear words as if whispered drifting by. I remember in them the Yaqui Indian village I had only imagined when I was a child.

4

New Vision Beginning

In day,
desert sounds were as winds
strung out past
old telegraph lines,
sighing, thrumming,
wind sounds stretched past infinity
and time beyond.

At night,
speckled planets slowed, stopped
came to unmoving silence,
and in that moment came
slow time,
time of this tale.

The first words in a new dream I the observer witnessed, spoke of Yaqui villages destroyed in 1900. How and why I shall write of shortly. Now, the words in the dream were coming, whispering as if in slow step with what lay ahead …

History is old,
old time that waits upon itself.
It is the voice of a mother,
subtly remembered, found
among the life and death of others
now grieved in threading memory.

In places, the white Sonoran desert
becomes a thin horizon,
holds images, ancient Yaqui villages
that magically remain.

There time nurses silent screams,
remembrances rising above hearing
to escape among low sand-struck hills,
agony that remembers year on year.

Listen to innocents' pain in death,
reweaving patterns and sounds of dying.
The dead make plaintive demands, entrap the mind,
then vanish among the twisting river canyons.
Left crying are the throats of children,
and women cry for all pain felt,
and the haunted screams of men are buried,
lonely and alone.

Otherwise all is silence on the far desert land
in the wail of a new wind rising off the Sea of Cortez
and the call of birds arriving and leaving.

I listened slowly. The coming dream's first faint words began receding, but returned with the vision. The dream returned in its own language, and I observed Teresa later that night.

5

San Ignacio

In the dream, I was there with Teresa, feeling through her senses. I remember her saying that there was one entry road that arced around from a highway into the hill village. Then it became the village's main paved road.

The road wound around a graceful plaza bordered with brooding trees and moved past rural people dressed simply, some bent and ancient. It continued past a church, monumental and worn, past uncrowded storefronts with worn benches next to open doors and moved by family rooms open to view. Further on, the orderly road branched onto dusty, rutted streets, their whitewashed adobe homes now plain without façade. Here roadways lacked adornment and held old rusted refuse—poverty with quiet simplicity, almost dignity. Finally, one branch of the roadway straightened and purposefully moved toward the town's solitary cemetery.

That resting place appeared without precise shape, old boundaries having deteriorated. Dimensions once set had been extended and altered incessantly. Crypts, mausoleums, nondescript plots crowded in all directions. At this goal, the road ended, facing sun-white statuary standing in benign isolation.

**Teresa spoke, remembering, waiting amid the white statuary,
feeling the desert wind quiet her body. She was entranced,
a fascinated child who hardly noticed tiredness or knew
physical movements, arms reaching upward as she heard her
own self, herself. Teresa, feel ancient prophecies. Here are
the people from whom you came ... you are of an old race ....
Join with me now in a new world, in this place.**

**Nothing more came, only mind words. Teresa only heard the
quieting
of mind and body, and slowly a sense of huge strength began
to form, coming from ground to air in this place at
the foot of the low mountain. The essence of strength was
embodied in a muted sound, swelling with persistent power.
Time, sun, and wind were outside of the strength that
grew and waited.**

**Teresa moved past the stone figures, past new forgotten
flowers, past crypts that wavered in the heat of the brilliant
sun. She walked back, back toward the abruptly rising
mountain that brooded over the cemetery.**

Strangely, the nondescript road had led to a seat of power that lay
somewhere beyond the gathering of cadavers, beyond a cemetery to the
base of a hill that quickly led onto a small, abrupt mountain. Looking up
she had to climb steeply to reach succeeding ledges not visible from
below. The climb seemed formidable. She looked back from higher up
onto the road that meandered off into paths that skirted the cemetery's
low back wall.

6

The Climb

I watched through Teresa's eyes, thoughts. Intent, she searched for a way up as her body struggled with unaccustomed angles. Eyes probed further, past old rocky resting places, perhaps ancient shepherd stations. Slowly a giant ledge emerged. It took high steps to reach it, and still her eyes rose higher. The angle steepened past more ledges; some appeared to be terraced layers of old burial sites. I felt Teresa's mind quieting from the exertion, reaching slowly beyond this rocky place. Her eyes returned to see below the faint paths she imagined filled with Indian children, women, and men, strong and feeble, descending from the mountain, moving toward a flowing river below—an ancient river bed was now dry and barren.

Teresa's eyes returned to map the climb: one path crossed the others, but all lead upward. Her mind followed the ancient lava stone that had tumbled down the mountainside. One path turned upon itself and suddenly resumed a direct climb. Her body was tired: legs quivered, breathing became deep, but still her mind rested in stillness.

Over the mountain, a new, brilliant sun lit up a yellow midmorning scene covering the valley. Surrounding hills and mountains cupped the town in somnolence. All appeared transfixed, immobile.

In the trance of the dream, Teresa leaned forward examining the land below. She saw the house she had departed from and heard the caws of large grey-black crows and grizzled hawks that wheeled up close and overhead. They seemed curious as they swept over the lone figure, examining, cawing and cackling, and grinding their beaks while skimming. Labored steps still moved upward as if drawn to the pale blue sky. Suddenly, the first signs of flat ground began to spread out leading to the top of the mountain. Teresa paused her slow motion then stopped.

**And in those moments of recovery there began
the emanations, a separate awakening of the climbing, aloof mind.
Senses became alert to a mild wind that moved small
mesquite bushes. The air was fragrant.
The musty-sweet smell of budding cactus rose from hidden,
rotting lineage. The wind quieted, emptying itself
further, leaving a pulsing serenity of spirit,
a vast tranquility. Nature sublime calmly focused
on itself, stretched, and drew up long, languorous rhythms.
Hearing and wind moved into a slow time.**

Saguaro, *Cholla*, Prickly Pear, and *Ocotillo* cactus rose from everywhere atop the mountain. The tallest, the *Saguaro*, stood with its thick, implanted strength showing in ridged, spiny imperviousness. Its roots clawed rock and invisible soil, sharing outcroppings and firmly resting on them. The thin, elongated *Cirio* mounted unlikely points and poses. Where the *Saguaro* was rooted in strength, the *Cirio* pirouetted, drooped flimsily, and feigned in repose, its flowery ends moving faintly in the surrounding air.

Teresa had reached a flat plain that lay atop the mountain. A jumble of rocks spread out before her, and one rock lay flat as a low table. She moved to it slowly and sat gently on its smooth surface. Immediately a transformation began.

7

The Vision

I watched as Teresa's whole composure changed from tired and searching to calmness and serenity. She became immobile, sat quietly on the rock, and listened as if hearing words spoken in another room. Later, Teresa understood that she was hearing messages moving between spirits, and that these words had no reality or accounting to them but were sounds carried place to place. Teresa learned that she was approaching a place of spirits, a spirit world lived by women.

A change from the outward reality of the mountain, the climb was becoming an inward trance like the deepest sleep. In this place Teresa was drawn to an earlier time, a reincarnation. She heard fragments of sounds from a gathering of foreign spirits drawn to a celebration. The spirits spoke in a language that all understood.

> *"I share with my sisters as we do in our mountain place, a fragment of memory from time past. It had been bitter cold on that narrow, English-built train making its way west from La Paz in the country of Bolivia. The train left near noon in hot sun. Two days later it was past Puno in the country of Peru, away from icy winds off Lake Titicaca and climbing toward Arequipa, straining to reach over icy places difficult to breathe in. The train reached a little station toward evening as the sky turned black.*

*"Nothing moved, passengers remained still, no one emerged
to board. I stepped off to talk to a crying child
sitting outside next to my rail coach. Together we
talked by the empty building in the charcoal night. And
the train unobserved moved away without a sound.
Still it was as planned. I remained and held the
child. We spoke of things.*

*"Bitter, bitter cold came in that still night.
Later a dim form of an Indian woman, the mother speaking
soft Quechua words, sat near us on the windless
side of a small, low wall. She spoke gently, and then
from inside her depth, another child cried. It wailed as if
echoing her reassuring words. Her sounds were with me all
that night of anguish, awaiting dawn, while cold moved
deeper, nearer to awesome pain. The children cried through
the hours; the mother returned from tiredness to tend the
sounds of hunger and cold. It was then I heard from a
painful place timeless in the earth, a small recreation
of its mystery. The children needed the sounds
and nurturing of their mother. And there I learned, never to
forget, that the same cold and hunger came to me.
The four of us remained transfixed until dawn came
with a slow brilliance, unaware, beginning anew.
The sun gave us warmth from the cold; the
night and icy winds gave the gift of pain
that we knew and never forgot
in days to come."*

Teresa sat feeling the smooth rock, its solidity, and its warmth. Momentarily the spirit sound stopped, soon followed by another. The following sound was softer, whispering of another place … of …

*"Sonoran Desert Mountains have majesty
as the Altiplano Mountains of the South, joined
one with the other as people belong together. The High Sierra,
magnificent ranges with the noon sun glinting off heavy white snows
that turn pale grey and ice blue as the white sun moves across their
brows.*

*"Sonoran Mountains, your quietness is the same, a way of
measuring vast silences between noises of thundering winds and of
nestling pale beauty in spring."*

And there the mind voice ended, and a new sound began to murmur
faintly, as if stirred awake by the earlier mind words of the Altiplano and
the Andes.

*I imagined as a child I had been in those
far mountains and in these where I am. Later, I sought
to describe to my son how, lying in the Sonoran Mountains,
the earth had the feel of the Andean coldness without
the pain-cold of the soul. The earth is the same earth
but for the coldness and such difference. The desert air atop this
place would feel cool then cold in either mountain place
under an alike brilliant sun—the whole remaining in
cloudless constancy. Without sun, the Andes and
the Sonoran Mountains are alike; only the pain of cold
differs. Nature, I tell you, is the same first
and only shows each of us a small difference.*

*Later in my spirit life, I recited something I told
my son of lying in the short stiff grass of the Altiplano
in one range of the Andes so close that the breaks
and curves of its peaks and jagged tops showed clear
waiting to be touched. Then the earth
began to give off a thrumming sound, a pulse as strong as
my own heartbeat, part of a vast power.*

I came to lay toward the four points with the center over me,
the sun white-orange, and there I first heard the
sounds of musical notes coming to me. A shepherd, a
young boy, passed close. I stayed half-raised in the grass.
He saw me and looked beyond. He did not intrude;
I had not asked. He only passed, followed by llamas and
alpaca, the human and animals moving in shadows in browns
and pale reds of cape and flapped hat. They moved together,
leaving plaintive musical sounds that mixed naturally
in an orange-yellow haze of light.

I knew later that I was called to lie there in prayer.
I lay near an early center of Indian belief, Tiahuanacu.
I had heard its sounds rising for a distance in the
high air. The boy likely came from there
to play his musical notes, to place his
self as being there. I was there with his acceptance when
he passed. Later, Tiahuanacu regained its respectful
quiet. The boy, having received my presence and carried
away his notes, left me in my own peace.

8

The Pledge

Again I watched as Teresa's mind returned from a deep place of sleeplike trance to feel the heat of the flat rock where she lay. Slowly her words began to form. She sat up, looking toward the flatter plain she had come to. Suddenly, I sensed Teresa feel a rush of thoughts coming as if separate from her person, as if from a spirit.

*Come, come to a like creation to the Incan peaks. Do
not sense difference. You and the mountains are one in the mind,
earth, rock, and spirit together. Absolute quietness
fills both, far from storms, wind, rain. Strength stirs in the center
of each, and sun coming over their presence calls
to drowsiness. The earth of pebbles and soil press on limbs
seeking downward, encircling. You are encircled as in the
womb of your mother, and you are the daughter that
I meet here.*

Teresa looked out, entranced by the sound. The mountaintop was desolate but for a soft caressing air moving over bushes and cactus placed in harmony.

Slowly, she rose feeling the air thickened in the warming sun, brilliant and intense, its light colorless as it entered her senses. The sun forced Teresa's eyes downward, near-closed against the brightness. Her eyes finally closed and remained blank, encased in the sensed pulsations and images first known upon awakening. Time passed, and it became dark again.

Teresa had entered into the vision of the world she
first visited as a young woman. The vision was in darkness, as
colorless as it had been light an instant before. Then evenly,
slowly, as miraculously subtle as light forming in daybreak, a
whiteness seeped into her eyes. It began
deep in the mind, a whiteness that came from an inside
self. The whiteness lighted shadows that became figures,
human figures moving dreamlike, limbs not touching surfaces.
The figures emerged from the four cardinal points and
downward
from a fifth vertical central direction. They moved easily in a
large circle that had a smaller inner one. The figures stood—
six, eight, ten, fourteen, then waited,
forming a circle of silence, silent friends in repose,
waiting to listen, to be instructed, present together.

In the innermost circle, suspended, stood a tall cactus,
a single huge trunk with two curving branches
flaring from its center. Slowly, evenly, the trunk began turning
to a pale green, its paleness moving upward to the curving
branches, and, imperceptibly, it became quartz with
slab-sided angular surfaces reflecting light, whitish light.
The cactus had become cast in crystal. Radiating
inner light, its inner substance reflecting on the
gathered figures.

Steadily the cactus held and pulsated light, still
and fixed. And the waiting figures began to move and bow
their heads to listen, moving as if hearing voiceless stories.
The scene was of slow pantomime, a recalling of events
recounted for each figure joined in the presence. And

a purpose permeated the silence awash in whitish light.
The figures each listened. From where her mind remained,
Teresa saw her figure stand among them and transfixed
listened to a sound telling of where she began.

The sound coming to Teresa was small, as from
the end of an echo, distant and yet clear and strong.
It said, "You have always been and you are a woman of
Seataka.
You are a Woman of Power in the world, and it is not a choice.
As you came in birth you were selected, and you are here
to tend to people, to their natures. You will protect them,
but you will change little of their nature. If each
is whole, each has choice to learn from what they do,
and each can change a choice. Your power is to lead, show,
protect from harmful choice, violence, and greed and to help them
find their beauty and peace through what they choose.
And you are charged to nurture new Women of Power.
So forever take your power, and they will find their own."

As I, the observer, watched with surprise, the now old figure of
Teresa slowly returned to sit on the flat rock. She appeared to awaken
slowly and to look about her with curiousity.

I noticed a change in daylight. Many hours had passed, and it was
near dark outside of the room. Teresa appeared very tired. She closed
her eyes again as she instantly saw that the huge cactus was gone, the
figures had left, and all sound had become silence. In their place stood
low, ordinary cacti surrounded by trodden-down, dry grass. The grass
formed an outer circle that enclosed a smaller one laced with ordinary
rock. Finally, I noted, nothing remained in her mind as she opened her
vacant eyes. Before long, there came a knock on the door and Juan's
voice called to his mother.

9

Story of Maria, Teresa's Mother

Best read are scraps of memory,
pieces infinitesimally scored
by diamond point intensity
on mirrors hung inside the head.

The following is my dream of Teresa's mother, Maria. Maria spoke of her life in Bacum, her Yaqui Indian village, and of other villages she played among that lay west of the Sierra Madre Mountains. The villages mostly adjoined the Yaqui River and the Sea of Cortez and were a part of the mythical land that lay in the Mexican State of Sonora.

Maria's words are relevant. It was through her tragic loss that Teresa's own life came to be. The upheaval in Maria's world began some time in the 1900s.

As a child in Bacum, life for Maria moved in slow, pleasant ways. Along with the rocky desert, there were green valleys where crops grew in stepped terraces among meadows of tall grasses that supported cattle and farm animals. There were stands of trees next to the Yaqui River, which lowered itself south to the dry, purple hill spines bringing high snow water into wrinkled desert crevices. Families in the villages bordering the river lived at a leisurely pace. On weekends they brought wagons to market loaded with corn, beans, squash, wheat, and many animals—cows, horses, mules, goats, chickens, and birds—all to sell and barter.

Maria remembered the springs and the gentle summer days spent with Panchito, her younger brother, exploring the forests and hills reaching up toward the snow of the Sierras. Greens and soft reds from desert plants covered their whole world. "No matter where we went, there was river water, meadows, and soft new grass," remembered Maria. "And Panchito was a good companion though he was slow and complained a lot."

Maria was almost fifteen, her brother Panchito was ten. She had a much older sister, Concha, although she was unsure how much older she was. Concha stayed home to help Guadalupe, their mother, which left Maria mostly free to play. Still Maria thought it unfair that she had Panchito to look after. But as long as he minded, Maria took him everywhere she went. They explored everywhere.

10

The Coming Attack

Now evenings had an earthen hum,
thrummed on reedy lines stretched thin,
strung to infinity.
Sounds pitched on sun blanched, whitening poles
marking out an empty desert,
holding swaying, sagging wires
entrusted with cryptic burdens.

Maria remembered the destruction that came to Bacum and other Indian villages and to the Yaqui people beginning about 1900. When it was over, Mexican soldiers, rural police, and Yankee cattle ranchers controlled the sprawling Yaqui grazing and farming river lands.

Maria was not sure when the attack began, but she recalled first coming upon soldiers and Indians she did not recognize when she was at play distant from the villages. She and Panchito watched as the soldiers shouted. Dark little men hurriedly dug holes in the sand and put up posts that looked like church crosses. Maria dragged Panchito closer to several soldiers. One, dressed in a big coat with gold stripes on his sleeves, was suspicious.

"What is it you two want?" he called out quickly.

"We, my brother and I, just wanted to see what you are doing."

"Well," responded the soldier roughly, "there is nothing to see so go away!" He moved off, finished with them. Meanwhile, Panchito had moved closer to another soldier and was looking excitedly at his huge, shiny rifle. Maria pulled him away, dragging him toward the nearest post. She was curious about what the posts were for. She wondered about the black line, like rope, being tied to the cross bars.

"Que son ... como se usan ... como?" she asked the nearest soldier. "What are they ... how are they used?" she asked. He, too, looked angry and seemed impatient but decided to talk, asking his own questions.

"Where do you live, and how old are you?"

"Well," she answered, "in the next village," and pointed northward. Then she repeated her questions.

He answered, "You remind me of my daughter, about your age, always asking questions and very curious." He stood shaking his head. "And those," he pointed to the scrawny posts with cross pieces at their tops, "those are just tree trunks with little pieces of wood on top to hold what are called a telegraph line. The black line is for the telegraph part."

"Oh," she said, "but what is a telegraph?"

He answered stiffly, "I've said too much, but the line carries sound like a drum, and the sound is heard far away at the other end of the line by someone who knows what the sound means. That's all I can say. It's time you went home!" With this the soldier turned to shout at the Indians.

Maria felt put off by his sudden gruffness but, still curious, turned to examine a post and a black line. She looked closely at one post; it was just a little thicker than her arm. The bark was peeled off, and the arm tied to the top held a single black wire. The posts and arms, she knew, came from forest trees cut down from the nearby foothills of the Sierras. These were playgrounds known to Maria and Panchito.

She walked away slowly with Panchito, still confused by what it all meant. Scolding him out of habit, she began to walk toward home, but soon she had to stop to look back. There stood the line of upright posts with their cross bars, holding the almost invisible black wire, all stretching back into the desert. Maria remembered thinking momentarily that after the color and beauty of the farmlands and tall grasses of the valley, the line of posts looked lifeless, out of place against their desert land.

11

The Attack

Later,
the arms hung mute on whitening posts,
sticks keeping a shallow foot in place,
gnarling upward toward new suns,
figures shuffling endlessly
to far, far mountains
on a trail ultimately lost, sad and empty,
gone beyond sight.

Maria, increasingly confused about the posts and their black wire, walked home with her brother with uncertain steps. She was unsure whether to tell Pa or the others of the mystery. They would ask questions, and she could only say what the soldier had told her. So Maria said nothing and warned Panchito to be quiet about the rifles or about wanting to be a soldier when he grew up.

However, Pa and Maria's mother, Guadalupe, had already heard about the soldiers from other people. They also wondered what the strangers were doing near the villages. At first, Pa wanted to go out to see what they were doing but did not have time. So little more was said. Maria and Panchito remained quiet.

The next day, a Saturday, was busy for all, including Maria. She was sweeping the street clean in front of their house when a man excitedly stopped his wagon nearby. He jumped off, waving his arms as he told a neighbor what had happened to him. His produce had been taken by the soldiers. As he talked, another wagon pulled up next to his with the same story. The soldiers were forcefully taking all wagons and animals coming into the market. They told the farmers they would be paid later by the Mexican government. Maria listened closely as other farmers told the same story. She quickly rushed into the house to tell the others, and soon Pa and her mother had rushed outside to join the crowd.

The presence of soldiers was unheard of at that time. In the past, the Yaquis had fought the Mexicans, but, except for a few old people, no one remembered the details.

The town leader soon came and told the farmers not to interfere with the soldiers. He said that he would dispatch a messenger to the central village to ask for news and advice. Most people slowly returned to their weekend, visiting around an empty produce market. A few sat and waited. By evening, the central village had sent no news, and life settled down to normal routines: male beer drinking and card playing and women gossiping.

At Maria's house, all was tranquil after the first excitement. By custom, Pa worked on Saturday. As a transporter of goods between the villages, he had mules to look after and wagons to repair. Always sensitive that his neighbors see him as responsible, he didn't drink and usually retired early. But, with all of the excitement, they all went to sleep later than usual. Pa and Guadalupe fell asleep first, followed by Concha who had the largest mattress in their common sleeping room.

That night, sleep came slowly to Maria. Not saying anything about the telegraph bothered her, and she felt worse after she heard gossip that townspeople had seen the strangers pulling a wheeled cannon on the road.

In the early morning, the attack against the villages began. Bacum was attacked first because of its place south of the other villages. Instantly the use of the posts and black line became clear to Maria. The soldier had said that the telegraph carried messages. And an important message to the soldiers was when to begin the attack! In the confusion that followed, Maria did not have time to think about anything more except how to escape the shooting.

As the village people learned later, the attackers included soldiers, federal rural police, and mercenaries hired by Mexican landholders and Yankee ranchers. The mercenaries attacked later, following the noise and confusion created by huge explosions that rained down on the town. The explosions killed many families outright. Houses were set afire forcing people onto the streets and increasing the chaos.

As the darkness lifted, Maria recalled hearing the deep cannon sounds and seeing puffs of smoke rising in the distance. The heavy explosions continued with shells raining down everywhere until most houses in Bacum had caught fire. The explosions created hails of shrapnel and flying brick and adobe. Maria remembered seeing people lying in pieces; the dead and dying were everywhere.

Somehow surviving men, boys, and women came out of nowhere, moving back to the southern end of the village where the fighting was expected. Earlier, they had learned of the soldiers and were certain an attack was coming. Some had heard of such attacks on the Yaquis from their grandparents. The old ones had endured much fighting the Mexicans, and the younger ones were preparing to do the same. Through the smoke and destruction, they carried old muskets, rifles, revolvers, and farm tools to build makeshift walls behind which they planned to meet the enemy.

At first they saw no attackers. But the cannon fire continued to fall everywhere, causing more destruction upon the closely packed houses. Then, slowly, as dawn broke, the cannon fire hit the main road and wagon trails leading north out of the village. It was also aimed at the houses on the main road to the south against which soldiers, police, and gunmen began to move into the village.

Meanwhile, the heavy cannon fire on the northern road prevented wagons and families from escaping. Seeing no escape, some returned to fight or to search for weapons and munitions to supply the waiting defenders. Some joined in building barricades behind which they could fight the invaders. Younger leaders screamed for the people to decide to leave or to remain and fight. Despite their hesitation, most able-bodied people, male and female, turned to stay and fight.

Other leaders moved about on the northern road helping old people and children gather household goods and food for departure. Their first goal was the western slopes of the Sierra Madre where in times past, Yaqui guerilla fighters had created hidden safe havens. Some leaders urged families to head for the border into Arizona where Yaquis had always found refuge.

At full daylight, Maria and her family heard that the attackers were advancing on all sides. They had been beaten back a number of times, and the townspeople had captured many guns and munitions, but the number of attackers and their new repeating rifles were overwhelming.

Pa, despite the confusion around him, had packed their main wagon with family goods and food. But he resisted leaving without helping his neighbors, especially the older people and their grandchildren. He distributed his remaining wagons and mules among them and helped them to load their belongings.

Left alone, Maria and Panchito had joined older children in digging and building barricades. During this time, Panchito slipped away; he had somehow gotten hold of a new rifle. Unseen, he hurriedly rushed off to hide it in the family's fully packed wagon.

Pa began to fear for his family and readied them to leave. Leading his most trusted mules and the one loaded wagon, he headed out onto the main road going north.

Just as he reached the road, a young leader ran up to the wagon warning him to continue fast so as not to be caught. He said attackers had gone around the village and people were being killed by the *yori*, the Mexicans. Some people were being captured, he said. Pa knew from talks with elders that capture meant lifelong captivity and hard slave labor in the tropical lowlands in Yucatan. The plantation owners, Pa had heard, paid much money for captives. So on hearing about people being captured, he quickly snapped at the mules, anxious to get beyond the main road as soon as possible.

12

The Escape

On the northern side some distance from the town, the main road split, with one branch going east more directly toward the Sierras. The other branch went north to the distant border.

The eastern branch quickly became clogged with fleeing families moving on foot or heavily loaded wagons. They chose this road to escape the flat plains and to get into the safer wooded areas. The attacking military commander must have quickly surmised this because soon after Pa got on the main road, cannon fire lessened there and became more concentrated on the branch road that was still some distance ahead. The wagons moving around Pa weaved constantly to escape falling shells and to get around holes in the road.

Several times, Pa stopped to move the dead and dying off to the side of the roadway. Maria noticed that he moved the dead bodies carefully, aligning their arms, legs, and shattered torsos so that they seemed to be resting or sleeping. None that he reached were left in awkward positions.

Some time later, Maria also noticed that Pa was getting tired. He had begun to act strangely. He looked around repeatedly and began to shout at family members and mumble to himself without making sense. Several times, he stopped the wagon as if preoccupied and suddenly came awake again to resume the trip.

Maria was afraid that the dangers facing his family were breaking her father. She could see it in his face and quick movements as he struggled with thoughts in his mind. Once he stopped, unmindful of the wagons traveling behind, causing them to go around his wagon. It happened at the split in the road going east. Absentmindedly, he began talking about their future to Guadalupe who sat next to him. By then, she too was concerned.

Maria listened as he asked his wife whether she would be able to feed the baby she was carrying. Guadalupe answered as calmly as she could, trying to make sense of his questions while urging him to go on. Finally Pa grew quiet and picked up the reins to join the rest moving eastward.

As the sun grew high, they passed isolated, muffled screaming coming from newly wounded and dying people hit by the explosions and shrapnel. Further back, they heard the dull sounds of gunfire, and it became clearer that Bacum was being overrun and that the remaining women, children, and old men were being killed or captured.

At times Maria noticed Pa looking back toward the rumbling sounds carried by the rising noon wind. She sensed his agony: as a responsible man he wanted to join his Yaqui brothers and sisters in defending their land but had instead decided to protect his family. He was leaving a people and home he had known all his life.

Toward evening, Maria could see Pa's heavy tiredness. He no longer talked to himself. Once he stopped and walked away from the wagon as if to urinate and was gone for what seemed a long time. Maria, concerned for his safety, asked her sister Concha to go with her to look for him. They searched and found him sitting on a rock staring at some birds and a rabbit. They called him, and he slowly returned to the wagon so they could continue on their journey. Toward nightfall, they stopped, and Guadalupe and Concha prepared their evening meal, careful to keep their fire low on Pa's instructions. Pa explained that they were in the desert, and fires could be seen for miles and might invite bandits. He did not join in further conversation. Panchito and Maria sat quietly, waiting to eat.

They quickly ate their meal of corn, tortillas, and beans, and no sooner were they through than Pa hurried them onto the wagon. Pa ordered Maria to walk alongside the wagon and said that Panchito would take her place later. It was nearing midnight when the wagon again clambered onto the hard-packed road and resumed its creaking way.

Maria remembered tying a short length of rope from her waist to the back of the wagon so as not to be left behind. She feared being lost in the darkness, so she walked close behind the swaying wagon. Soon she felt the tug of the rope as she fell behind. In her drowsiness, she relived her pride in Pa, how even in his grief and fear he helped the dead to agonize less.

Sometime in her reverie Maria awakened from her sleepwalking by her brother's low voice. He had been ordered to sleep early atop the wagon so that he could take the reins in the morning. "Climb up," he whispered as he reached for her. "Take my shoulder, hold on, raise yourself, pull. Climb on and take my place." After she pulled herself up he gave up his seat, made room, and held her. "We'll take turns sleeping until Pa calls me."

The desert night had turned very cold, and soon Maria was lost in sleep next to the warmth of Panchito's small body. Slowly the darkness of the moonless night had enveloped all including the dim forms of a few wagons strung out in a lonely entourage. Pa's wagon continued moving in its slow way, simply plodding along east and north toward the Sierras.

For some time, the old man had been in a kind of trance bound to the rhythmic swaying of the wagon. Only occasionally did he manage to escape the returning circle of sleep to see the small patches of reality he tried to hold on to. He shook his head to peer into the dark road ahead, in an altered wakeful state momentarily, only to drop into sleep again. He half-dreamed through an agonizing weariness of having failed his village by fleeing. He experienced a cowardly exhilaration in being free from the death around him, and yet felt an awful sadness in cutting his ancient bonds with home. The sleeping part of him drifted through lightening clouds. But another part of him moved with the mules in deep, rhythmic swaying to the sounds of creaking leather and the straining joints of wood.

The wagon moved on, unknowingly falling back from the group until deep in the night when a fate the old man had not planned on began to unravel.

Unknown to the souls in the wagon, they were alone. Pa's tired mules had plodded on obediently, mile after mile. Caught up in their own tired stupor, they were no longer aware of guidance from the reins. While unsupervised, they had followed a new fork in the road. The wagon had moved casually onto a sandy trail that went mostly south, into the heart of the Sonoran Desert and toward the interior of Mexico. They continued on this path hour after hour, throughout the darkest parts of the night.

13

The Bandits and Rape

Pa awakened abruptly. The wagon had stopped. It was early, and the beginning rays of the new sun came into his eyes and awakened him. Quickly looking around at the mounds of sand then squinting into the sun, he knew what had happened.

"Guadalupe, Maria, Concha," he shouted, "we have lost our way … We're going into Mexico, not east and north!"

The others, forced from their sleep, quickly responded. Without waiting, Maria and Panchito jumped down to stand by the wagon and moments later were ordered back onto it by Pa. He climbed atop the driver's seat to look at the trail and then scanned the surrounding mounds for movement. Before he had finished searching, the distant figures of several horsemen appeared. They came suddenly from out of the near sandy mounds. Pa studied them, and as they came closer, he could make out that there were four—three grown men and what looked like a boy of fifteen. The four kept coming in a slow, easy manner heading straight for the wagon. Before they reached the wagon, Pa scrambled down from the seat and stood next to the mules.

"*Buenos dias, senores,*" Pa said, speaking hesitantly. As the horses reached them, one stepped off his saddle adorned with silver inserts and kept his eyes on Pa without answering. The tallest of the four, he wore a large bandolier of rifle shells strapped across his chest and seemed to be the leader. He faced Pa.

"*Si, buenos dias, y quisas vienen solos?*" he asked harshly as if demanding to know if they came alone and whether they had seen other wagons or people.

"No, we have traveled all night and did not see anyone, and we came alone," Pa answered. Maria remembered her father sounding humble and soft-spoken before the strangers. Earlier, he had removed his sombrero as a sign of respect.

"No, *senores*," he added directly, "we come alone and maybe we are lost because we wanted to go east and north and now we are only going east, and, no, we have not seen the people you ask about."

He remained standing next to the wagon, clutching his sombrero as the tall man walked his horse over to stand next to the mules. "You have good animals here. What do you have in the wagon?"

Pa left the wagon and stepped toward the mules before answering. "We have little except things for the family for our trip, a little food, water, some clothes, a few things."

"And," added the tall man with a sneer, "you have some women!"

"*Bueno*, yes," Pa said reluctantly, "they are my daughters, my wife, and son, all I have left of my family." Pa's voice dropped, sounding strange, almost pleading. It was a sound Maria had not heard before. Pa spoke directly to the tall man as if trying to keep attention on himself and away from the others. "You are welcome to food, and I have a little money that I brought for the trip."

The tall man kept looking at the wagon as Pa spoke. "Well," said the man in an offhand way, looking closely at Maria, "we'll take the money an' guns if you have any. But," he continued, "just don't make any wrong moves."

As the man spoke, Pa reached for his money belt tied under his blanket. The tall man hesitated then reached for his holstered gun. Thunderous, collapsing sounds followed that remained deep in Maria's memory. Pa had been shot.

As the bandit fired, Panchito, sitting atop the wagon, reached for his hidden rifle. He grabbed it, raised, and pointed it awkwardly at the gunman who quickly faced the boy. In a split instant there was a new round of gunfire, this time hitting Panchito and coming from all of the grown gunmen. The boy, hit repeatedly, simply fell over dead. Pa also lay crumpled up next to the wagon while Guadalupe and the two girls sat paralyzed.

Immediately the tall bandit began shouting to the others. "*Vengan ...* come on, you cowards. We've got ourselves some women!"

Grinning, an older, heavyset one dropped off his horse, followed by a younger, surly faced one. The boy, frozen in position, remained mounted. Ashen faced, he held rigidly to the pommel of the saddle, still seemingly shocked by the shooting.

Concha meanwhile quickly slipped unnoticed off the side of the wagon and began running hard toward the mounds of sand until the tall one caught sight of her. "Stay with the wagon," he shouted as he remounted his horse and quickly gave chase. Moments later he returned dragging Concha by a noose around her neck. She was gasping as he released the rope and called to the surly one. "Tie her up or have with her while I have the young one." He then turned, shouting to the older man who was already trying to catch and hold Maria. "Look, old man, you stand back and watch how it's done. Later it's your turn."

Maria remembered what followed in detail. She described it in the dream I had later. In the dream, she sounded as if she had been standing apart observing what was happening rather than living it.

The thin child sobbed and screamed piercing, hurtful sounds as the tall man lay heavily on her chest. Then she lay whimpering, sounding like a trapped, exhausted animal. She began screaming again as he tore at her clothes and began to force himself upon her. The screams lodged, muffled in her throat and mixed with other cries and words that were unable to burst through the fright and pain.

Maria described knifing pain gagging her breath. Somewhere, somehow, she remembered glimpsing herself as dead and then dark moments of pain mixed with slivers of sharp, white light crashed into her eyes. She dimly recalled her clothes being torn off of her body, and the brown, sweaty face of the man. She felt the distant pounding and heaving weight of his half-dressed body suspended over her. Later, the older man smelled fowl, with acrid sweat and a breath that Maria would never forget.

She remembered the boy thrown against her thin body and feeling momentarily, through all the violence, that he would not harm her. She recalled at first that he was not much bigger than herself and somehow looked like Panchito. At first, it felt almost like when she and her brother struggled in play. She felt only old pain and waited for the nightmare to lift. Soon the boy recoiled from her body, but the agony continued.

Shouting arrogantly, the tall bandit lifted the boy's weight off of Maria and began calling her "*puta, puta* ... whore, whore!*" He kept repeating the words in savage anger while again preparing to fall upon her. Then he struck her methodically, becoming more enraged. He continued hitting Maria repeatedly with his huge fists while the other two grown men joined in, cursing and hitting her, twisting her body when she screamed. One squeezed her barely formed breasts and face when she resisted.

Throughout the attack on Maria, Concha had been tied and gagged; she opened and closed her eyes in horror.

The raping and beating of Maria continued for a time, done in turn by all three grown men. She escaped into a deep unconscious state where she only heard the harsh, ugly laughter mingling with brutish anger. In her escape, she felt less of the bodily pain they continued to inflict. From this distant sense of time Maria dimly came to understand what she later shared in the dream that reached me.

Maria later knew of men releasing stored hurt and hatred toward women for their dependence on their ability to nurture. Men could also nurture but not as freely and only for purposed ends. Men could not admit this and instead felt anger.

Finally, Maria no longer resisted. She lay still, retreating further into a secret place where children go when living in deepening fright. But she recalled fiercely not losing consciousness. She only lay as if dead, cradled by her shocked mind.

In time the three grown men gave up arguing whether to kill the survivors. They agreed to take Concha but were unsure of what to do with the older, pregnant woman and Maria. The fat bandit who had been the most brutal talked of killing the two women. Maria heard him argue the loudest, his words of death reaching deep into her. Then the tall one argued that they would die anyway in the desert.

The fat one countered, "Alive they can accuse us sometime!"

"But," said the other, "they'll die out here, and besides I can't kill that way, shooting women."

Finally the fat man agreed, "*Bueno, vaya*, leave them to die an' it's time we left here."

Distantly Maria heard the buried movement of boots in soft sand, and from somewhere came Concha's muted screams. Kicking and screaming, she was lashed to the pommel of a saddle. Mixed in were sounds of the men's continuing arguments and the occasional laughter. Then there was a softer movement of horses as they began riding off. Only Concha's muffled screams were heard, and these also ended in silence.

Afterwards Maria lay still for a long time. She felt limp, immobilized, without strength, a crumpled heap. She remembered her eyes closing and falling into a deep sanctuary, embraced in timelessness.

14

Maria's Survival

The lost time seemed to last seconds. Then Maria returned to feeling the desert heat and seeing the white sun hovering through afternoon clouds. All was blank and empty. Suddenly, freezing fear intruded as she recalled Concha's screams. She felt panic coupled with deep, enveloping pain. Her sides burst with sharp hurt; breathing came with agonizing effort. Maria tasted blood deep within her mouth and imagined it flowing from her head. She felt encased in heat and locked in unmoving pain. Her lips had frozen tight, and her closed eyes dimly allowed light to filter through.

Images floated inside her mind in wavering, twisted ways. Amid a pounding nausea and fright, a returning urgency about something kept appearing. She felt the sensations of earlier panic and heard men arguing far off as if they had returned. At times, their voices came closer, and she wanted to stop her fright to keep from trembling and to keep them from hurting her again. She kept her eyes rigidly closed to escape the terror and the fear that they would return. They would, Maria feared, force the boy to rape her. She imagined the bandits mounting their horses and cantering away toward the east, rifles glinting in the bright desert sun. Then Maria fainted, dropping away into her sanctuary.

Her small body lay in pained sleep for hours. Nothing stirred around her as the intense sun inclined west toward the sea and distant ocean. Memory, time, mind—all were pain now, whole, complete, covering. Nothing remained that was not pain in her inner body, arms, head, face, and eyes. The numbness in her groin was beyond physical pain. Needle-sharp feelings broke through to stab and clamp themselves around her stomach, legs, and lungs, stifling her breathing. Maria could taste the heavy, almost nourishing tang of her own blood.

Desert time passed beyond Maria, gently darkening. Within her, images formed. She watched herself arriving in small, crumpled form and waiting there for hours. She hardly knew the details of the tragedy engraved in her mind; it would take years for them to manifest.

Time passed; dark hours became lighter. The desert scents created by the white-hot sun lingered, awaiting morning. In the new small light, Maria's mind struggled to find its way back to outer life, still fearful of being noticed or causing movement. She opened puffed, distorted eyes to peer into a faint morning light. All was quiet except a gentle moaning coming from somewhere. Maria moved to raise herself and look: all was empty, without feeling or life. The world had become silent with still air and blank desert. Mutely, she retreated, surrounded by bits of mixed cloud and sky.

She watched herself flee, escaping from monstrous spirits, recoiling demons, and serpents. The creatures sprang from childhood dreams, rising from low ominous clouds that stretched across her view. The forms rose from among the deep grasses of her village foothills, rose with the trembling steps of giants and shrieks of victims, horrors believed and exchanged among the very young. And the creatures devoured her body even as she twisted and screamed to escape. The terror never seemed to leave. In one scene, all receded to a point and moved with her flight from accompanying terrors and devouring forms.

The pulsing scene mixed with momentary intuitions of being held and nurtured by her mother. Images crossed, recrossed, and formed again. Terror was replaced with warmth; fear of pain and dying was soothed by her mother's sounds coming to Maria from far off. Maria heard distant, reassuring words like those heard before awakening from the most fearful dreams.

Again, torn loose, Maria crossed a chasm of darkness, a gorge of blackness. And again there came a seeping of gentle feeling, a soft movement. Suddenly, enlarging white circles of light spun out from where Maria lay and centered in her eyes.

Plaintively, words came from her dear mother who cradled and rocked Maria and talked to her limp, bruised body. Somehow Guadalupe had wrapped Maria in her threadbare, worn *reboso*, the often restitched shawl that had swaddled each of her three children in their time.

"I have been waiting for you for many, many hours, afraid you were not returning to me. Still I knew you would." Maria looked up, watching her mother through clearing eyes. Strange how old Mother looked, ancient. "Maria, you are what is left to me. My husband killed, Panchito killed, my Concha taken from me. We two are left of our family. Nothing more, and I waited and waited, afraid of losing you and now I thank my God you are back."

Free to cry, the old woman held Maria close, her tears slowly falling on her old *reboso* as she gave thanks in her Yaqui dialect. Maria dozed again, freeing herself from the nightmares forming earlier. The terror was lifting. But nightmares and pain remained.

15

Resuming the Journey

My words—those of the observer—feel awkward. After I felt Maria's inner world during and after the rape, I also experienced a strange dream that seemed to tell Maria of her coming fate. It was as if she had learned something of her daughter-to-be, Teresa. Or perhaps the dream that I observed meant that Maria should know of her future child. Whatever was intended I could only attest to what came through in the subsequent dream episode. Maria's return to her mother was accompanied by a subsequent dream—a gathering of silence from which sound had been removed.

A far ring of dimming colors lingered, stretching as if flung outward from some cauldron heated by the sun. The coming evening pulsed with giant fire, like the dying down of burning coals had left streaks across the sky, reflections settling on the western reaches of the eye.

Maria traveled empty miles as she lay in the warm desert air, feeling far from home, wrapped gauzelike in bits of memory. She heard words that became feelings and said, "Woman is the tree of life. She is sacred. Woman's womb is the path of the creator, and the moment of conception is as close as you come to his work. You are known by what you do, not what you say." The thoughts paused.

"First, male and female spirits unite as spirit
life begins with the unborn. Here is love, joy
that grows in a woman. Then creation is complete
in time, space, in all that exists. Here is good in self
as evil. Here is both, to know and choose in life.

"Each knows the other and respects each.
Suffering, then, comes from each side.
From a center of each, they have conflict in silence.
And there is conflict until we choose."

At that moment I observed Maria listening closely, trying hard to understand.

"You come from believers in four past worlds,
beyond knowing each part had an end.
Then each world ended with struggles of the good and fruitful
with destructive ones. Then little was left.
You are a part of a fifth world of five senses.
Here are choices of time and growing of a large spirit.
Here choices await a far sixth world of senses
aided by women of Seataka. Then Lord of Dawn and bright
moving stars, of art and golden works of peace and love,
of unity and honesty, arrives. Rootless people moving
somewhere to somewhere that seek light from stars
will change longing to reality. There will be silence
for each choice, a time unknown,
a mystery coming to a deeper self."

It was as if the message and voice were ending. Thereafter Maria slipped further into a deeper, lonelier silence, her face perplexed, her mind seeking to understand.

16

Therapist's Respite

At one point, I sensed the dreaming was suspended. I felt as if the dreams had not happened, as if the people had not existed. Life and sleep returned to normal. For a time, I resumed counseling clients with marital, family, and individual mental-health problems without interruption.

When the dream episodes first began, I postponed or cancelled my appointments to avoid contaminating my professional work with this emerging content. I did not discuss anything connected to the mysterious dreams with anyone. The visions I had seemed too personal, too confidential—not unlike the information that came to me in my professional role. Until this writing, I felt as if I was simply entrusted with the information. Intuitively, I felt an obligation to relay nothing until somehow released to do so. I had the sense that what I observed had not been completed, which I later found out was indeed the case. Still, the dreams suspended and then resumed after a break. I caught glimpses of Teresa and her family followed by longer episodes. Sometimes I saw disjointed segments, sometimes orderly views of the tragic journey.

The first glimpse to return began suddenly after a night of heavy sleep. Toward early morning, I witnessed Maria's thoughts. In the dream, Maria awakened to the sounds of her mother praying over the bodies of her husband and son after the tragedies that had befallen them on their journey and before they resumed the trip to Casas Grandes.

17

The Burial

In dim memory, Maria felt her body carried to the shade away from a harsh desert sun. She wavered between full and semi-consciousness. Alone, Maria revived as the air turned hot, forcing her to rise feebly, holding to the spokes of the wagon wheel. She looked about.

Much earlier in morning darkness, Maria faintly remembered seeing two figures laid out next to the road. They still lay there in the hot sun, while her mother spoke over them. Her voice had broken through to awaken Maria.

Now, her body burning with pain, Maria felt an urgent need to go toward the figures. She slowly dragged herself toward them and upon reaching her mother, quickly saw the exhaustion and pain etched on her aged face. Guadalupe was months pregnant with her fourth child, and the tragedy that had fallen on her family was taking its toll. Still, through early and late morning, she had been busy preparing the bodies of her husband and Panchito for burial. While Maria had lain unconscious, her mother had rubbed the blood from her husband's face and had dressed both in clean white shirts and peasant trousers. She prayed over them.

Papi especially appeared composed, wrapped in a serene dignity that Maria had seen on the dead in the village—free from the pain of dying. Panchito, dressed in his best white clothes, also lay in quiet repose as if asleep.

Maria noticed her mother had covered the bodies, but for the faces, with stones she found on the road. Guadalupe sat spent, deep in thought. Maria waited quietly and soon moved to her side. Shortly, her mother began to talk as if in conversation, as if her husband and son were alive and listening.

> *I am with Maria. Concha has been taken from us.*
> *Now Concha is in our prayers. Now we are left to create*
> *memory places of you, my husband, and you, my son.*
> *And before you leave to move with spirits in the*
> *quiet of the earth, we need from each a part of the self*
> *to give to our coming child.*

As Guadalupe finished speaking she reached for the head of each and removed strands of their hair. She held the hair high, pressed these to her heart, and continued speaking.

> *These bindings enclose a family. Woman*
> *who bears or keeps another's child keeps the memory*
> *in the strands that connect us all. The strands*
> *make a place for each death and each coming of a*
> *child to a family. Thereby the circle is made*
> *and kept for all time, and our mother is to keep it so.*

Maria had heard the Yaqui prayer as a child. When Panchito came, he was told, "A child born, grown old, and turning to death is blessed with a lineage woven into a history of an enlarging family and its people. Thereby each member shares in memories of the whole loving circle, unbroken between all. The cycle of life, death, and change happens in the family as long as the circle endures."

Maria nodded, hearing the words from far off and again became enclosed in darkness. She remained there, sleep closing off her mind, and sometime later awoke, shrieking, "Mother!" In her sleep, she had gathered strength, and this time her cry carried anger as if she were just awakening from the attack. Her face contorted as she bolted upright,

45

shrieking, "Mother"! Suddenly moving with strength and purpose, Maria called out stridently and harshly, "Mama!"

Frightened, her mother stood up from where the bodies lay as Maria continued shouting. "I am here my child," she responded gently, "What is it?" As Guadalupe watched, Maria suddenly rose to her feet and spoke as if Pa were speaking.

"Mother, I am now ready, and as soon as we can, we must leave on our journey to find your sister. There is no more time to wait or waste." Maria continued talking in a strong, steady voice. "We must leave. So let the bodies where they are. Papa and Panchito are dead, Concha is gone, and nothing will change that. Now let us go on ... I will feed the mules a little of what is left of our corn and water and harness them so we can leave before the sun goes down. It will be dark, but we'll find our way!"

Guadalupe began to move toward the wagon unsteadily on hearing Maria's harsh voice. She was suddenly afraid of her daughter. The anger in her voice sounded like that of her husband when he was angry.

"Yes," she replied quickly, "I will be ready as soon as I am through with the burial."

Maria, recognizing her harshness, continued more softly. "Father and Panchito are dead, and now I must decide what we will do if we and the baby are to live. Mama, I love you, but I will decide what is best to do, and we must leave soon to find people or a village where we can be safer."

Soon Guadalupe, having covered the bodies with stones she had collected, wearily moved to the wagon. With much effort, she climbed to her place on the front seat. Maria, after feeding and watering the mules, harnessed them and clambered onto the other side. Without saying a word, she began to head the wagon onto the road. The mules, though still tired, pulled steadily as evening came. Soon all was in darkness as the lonely wagon continued its trek on the sandy road heading north and somewhat east. Guadalupe fell asleep, and Maria held her closer.

18

Journey Resumed and Casas Grandes

Steadily, the wagon moved in darkness with Maria occasionally talking to the mules as her father had done. More and more, she felt the need to take the place of her father in looking after the both of them. While she was preoccupied with peering ahead for signs of strange activity, she was also becoming concerned that her mother would fall ill.

Once her mother awoke with a start, jarring Maria from her tiredness. "Mama, I know you are tired and not feeling well, so we will stop for a while so that you can rest from all this moving." Maria brought the wagon to a stop and held the near-empty goatskin to her mother's parched lips. "I will move you to the back of the wagon so you can sleep stretched out in the old clothes." Slowly she helped Guadalupe over the seat, and soon her frail body was lost among the baskets and clothes. "You rest, and later I'll start a small fire. Maybe there is something left to eat."

Maria waited patiently until she could hear her mother breathing deeply. She sat on the wagon seat, dozing. After a short time, she again took up the reins and slowly returned to the roadway, talking softly to herself and to the mules.

"We cannot stay out here with a fire that can be seen and far from people, so we have to go on until we find a house." The journey continued in the dark early morning hours.

Finally daylight began to emerge and the world around them became real. Maria had gradually felt colder as the night progressed but had ignored its slow effects on her body. Now, as she looked about from the wagon, she recognized where their journey had taken them. They were in a higher place surrounded by big trees and a colder climate on the western side of the Rocky Mountains. It was frigid, and neither Maria nor her mother had warm clothes to withstand the cold. Soon Maria began to hear Guadalupe cough, and by the time Maria found a favorable place to stop and to attend to her, her mother was shivering. Despite being wrapped in their old clothes, she had caught a dangerous fever. Nothing could warm her, even Maria's body heat as she held her close.

The early daylight hours passed. Maria fell asleep holding her mother. She awoke in the early afternoon to find Guadalupe's lower body covered in blood. Guadalupe was incoherent, mumbling, and delirious. Terrified, Maria searched for the tiny fetus. Guadalupe's baby had arrived stillborn.

As the observer, I could only surmise the extreme sadness felt by Maria following the death of her future brother or sister. Although I do not know for sure, it is likely that Guadalupe carried out the burial of the fetus following a secret ritual. Another sad burial had taken place somewhere by the side of a road as they continued on in search of the mother's sister.

I will continue to describe what I observed as faithfully as I can, even though I only caught glimpses of some matters.

Ultimately the lone wagon reached the outskirts of a town. It was not Casas Grandes where they planned to stay with Guadalupe's sister, Esther. The sisters had not been close and had always quarreled. The younger sister Esther had always felt that Guadalupe was favored by their parents. So as a young woman, she had left Bacum and had not been heard from for a time. Eventually Guadalupe and her family learned that Esther had settled in Casas Grandes. Esther once notified them that she was well and would visit Bacum. However, they heard nothing more until an acquaintance of hers visited Bacum and told them about Esther's life. It had been difficult: her husband beat her, and she had to work to support her family. Beyond that nothing was known, even whether Esther would want to see Guadalupe.

Maria was aware of the problem between the sisters, but in time on the journey she forgot. Instead she was trapped reliving the rape, the attack on her family, and the earlier attack against her home in Bacum. The strong anger she first felt intensified as they met people on the road.

Several times Maria almost had to beg for food and water. She always offered to work for assistance; she sometimes washed dishes or clothes. Mostly, however, Maria felt she was turned down because she appeared too dirty and could not be trusted. She heard insulting remarks about not using Indians for housework near the family's children. The anger she felt combined with the hurtful physical reminders of the rape.

Particularly during long night hours alone the terror preyed on her mind. She began to have nightmarish thoughts of wanting to punish others, of being vengeful. Several times, forgetful of her sleeping mother, Maria began to cry out her thoughts. And several times Guadalupe awoke with a start on hearing the screams of her daughter. Once her mother had asked her to stop and join her in prayer. She listened as her mother's wavering voice still weak from fever recited prayers. Maria listened, but she knew with certainty that she no longer believed in them.

Maria worked in several homes for food, water, and corn for the mules before arriving in Casas Grandes and was feeling increasingly hostile. She felt insulted by the stares of people they encountered on the roadways. She felt their disgust when she stopped and asked for incidental help regarding her mother's condition.

Maria felt this prejudice after another long day on the road when they stopped to ask for water for the mules and themselves. A local finally and reluctantly gave them water but nothing else. Maria spoke angrily to her mother. "These Mexicans," she interrupted herself to spit into the road, "think they are helping poor, lost Indians who can't even speak Spanish." Maria spat again, "But they are the ignorant, lazy ones … and I spit on all of them!" Guadalupe tried to reason with her, but Maria only became angrier until she was almost crying. Afterwards,

Maria's anger prevented her from talking to her mother or offering her comfort for hours. Maria was withdrawing, and Guadalupe felt a strong need to speak about her continuing anger.

"I know you are angry with all things. What has happened to us is wrong. Our peaceful village should not have been attacked, nor our families, nor should the killings happened, nor the loss of Concha, nor my child dying, nor the attack on you." The frail woman struggled to get her breath then spoke in a whisper.

"Yet now the best we can do is to continue as we can … and to leave being angry because then we destroy what is left of our lives." With that Guadalupe lay back and closed her eyes.

Maria listened quietly. She had stopped the wagon, and suddenly she began to laugh, to stamp her feet, and to cry out to no one in particular.

"What is there to live for? They have destroyed what we had—home, my father, brother, and sister, even your stillborn child. And they destroyed me!" Maria choked and paused, her eyes suddenly drenched in tears.

"I told myself I would not cry and instead to stay angry so as not to forgive or forget." She turned to her mother who seemed to be asleep and continued speaking in a menacing voice. "Yes, I will feel angry at these Mexicans as I work and serve them to get scraps from their table. But they are the enemy, and I will not forget that they destroyed our lives and brought us to this."

Though her eyes had been closed, her mother had been listening. She raised herself to speak softly. "We must not attack these people—none we have seen are soldiers or rich people. They are farmers like us. They did not attack us so how can we be angry with them?"

The words of understanding seemed only to enrage Maria who turned, half rising from the wagon seat. Glaring, she shouted, "If you were not my mother I would never want to talk to you again. You talk like a fool who never learns from being hit and being made less of. Those who attacked us were like these people we've met, and we cannot forget what they have done. I am sorry to hear you talk like that, and you can do what you want, but me—I will stay angry so as to hate them more!" Maria turned abruptly, dismissing her mother.

Guadalupe, tears streaming down her lined face, moved to get onto the wagon seat. She struggled with her balance but finally pulled herself onto the bench. Maria watched angrily, making no move to help her mother. Seated, Guadalupe turned to her daughter. "Maria, I thank the spirits for bringing you back to me. Know I love you and will always love you and care for you as I can. Now we must still journey together, carrying remembrances of our family that we cannot forget."

She paused for a time. "I am so sad," the bent old woman continued. "I listen and hear what you say in anger ... and still I know that it is left to us to live as we can and to stay well and to be warmed by what we do."

Maria remained still, listening, unmoving. After a time, she snapped the reins for the mules to continue their patient pulling. Time passed on the road. Finally Maria stopped the wagon and this time turning to Guadalupe, reached for her hand. She looked at her mother intently, her face now relaxed. Gently she held her mother's hand, waited, and spoke softly. "I am deeply sorry for what I said. I love you my mother, and I am sorry that I shouted at you with words of anger. I am finding it hard to be kinder because of the great anger that comes over me. Maybe one day the anger will be finished, and you will not hear it." She looked into her mother's face again. "But know that I am never angry with you because we have each other forever."

Toward evening, they came to a small farmhouse with several lean-to outbuildings and corrals. Maria, tired but in better spirits, approached the outdoor family kitchen.

"Yes, you can stay for the night," said the stout young woman surrounded by several children. "I can use a little help with clothes, but only after you and your mother have eaten." As the woman spoke, she looked closely at Guadalupe, "I'll help her down and place a mat for her, and later we can bring her food. Maybe now she needs quiet and sleep." She turned to quiet her children. "They will stay away from your mother. And you may come with me, and together we can talk and wash clothes."

After helping Guadalupe onto a torn but clean mat, Maria turned to help with the wash. The woman gave Maria coffee with goat's milk for both her and Guadalupe then turned to wash a basket of clothes. She had much to say about their farm life and her husband who often had to travel to sell the little produce and chickens they raised.

"Carlos is so good and patient with me if I talk too much. He is a good man, and we are happy as you can see with our five children ... and much wash." Elena was her name, and she laughed easily.

"So tonight you will stay here, and then if you wish, you can leave early in the morning light. By then your mother should be rested and ready for the journey. Carlos knows the roads and will tell you about getting to Casas Grandes the quickest way. He will return tonight." As she finished speaking, they heard noise from the roadway. The children had seen the wagon of their father and had rushed to greet him.

"There he is now," the woman called out. She quickly moved to meet the wagon and to get the children out of the way of the mules. "We have company, and they will stay with us." Turning to Maria and her mother, she introduced them. "They have had a difficult time since leaving their village, and I will tell you later about what they have told me."

Carlos, a small wiry man, quickly jumped off the wagon and extended his hand to Maria and acknowledged the old woman. "I am glad Elena, my wife, was here to help, and I am at your service." Saying this, he removed his sombrero and picked up the youngest of his children. "I too have been a long time on the road though likely not as long as you two, and I was fortunate to sell all the produce I took so we shall eat well." He lifted a bag, a shank of burlap covered meat from the front seat, and a jug of wine and escorted by his children made his way into their simple lean-to kitchen.

"As Elena says, you will eat supper with us, then after breakfast you can take some food and water for the trip. I expect that you would be going to Casas Grandes, which is not far now and on this road." Carlos paused and studied Maria and the old woman. "I hope you do not think me rude, but you," nodding to Maria, "remind me of my young sister whom I would want to protect. So I would say to continue steadily on the main road and not take side roads because they can be dangerous. I will give you an old sombrero, and Elena can give you one of her old scarves so that you can tie up and hide your hair. Then if you move steadily, you'll be there very soon!" Carlos also said he would put up, feed, and water the mules.

Later Carlos, speaking mostly to Maria, continued. "My wife has spoken of you and your mother and of where you come from. I have been to Bacum, your village. It is very green maybe because of your river. It's not like our land that is almost desert. And you were fortunate not to try to cross the Sierra Madre before this. It cannot be done by wagon but mostly by climbing. Here the mountains turn to foothills and further north these are easier to cross, especially going east." Maria listened quietly to Carlos, surprised that he offered the information so easily.

"So when you leave, stay to the right of the sun." Carlos showed what he meant with his body. "Very soon you will come to Fronteras. Then you turn east toward the sun and after a time ask people where Casas Grandes is, which is nearby. Just ask people; they will tell you where to go. And as you go, keep getting water for you and for the mules because it is hot, the desert. Also, as I said, always stay on the main road and do not take any of the small roads. Then you will be safe."

At first, Maria's response to Carlo's words was one of withdrawal. She did not know what to say. Later she expressed embarrassment for being so quiet and not thanking him earlier. After eating they quickly retired but not before Carlos had again explained about the roadways.

In the morning it was still dark when they heard Carlos harnessing and feeding the mules. He talked in a low voice. Maria began to rise and to awaken Guadalupe. "Soon," said Maria, "we should be on our way." Even as she spoke, Elena was setting out breakfast.

Shortly, Carlos came in and took his place at the small table and again began reminding Maria and Guadalupe of the right roadway to take. "I have known bad people on the small roads. There are bandits out there, so one has to be careful. But I have faith that you will soon reach Casas Grandes." He smacked his lips as he ate his tortillas and eggs, "So be calm; God will be with you and your mother." Minutes later he got up and left to work in the corral.

Shortly, too, Guadalupe settled in the back of the wagon, and Maria stood ready with the reins. At the last moment. Elena reached up and handed Maria a basket of food for their lunch and supper. "It is little," she said modestly, "but it is what we have to share." As Maria reached for the basket, tears filled her eyes. How could this couple be so kind? She felt unable to speak. "Too," added Elena haltingly, "I've watched and can tell your mother is very weak and becoming sick. It would have been good if you two could have stayed longer so she could rest more. As soon as you reach Casas Grandes have her in bed and resting."

Maria was taken aback by the words about her mother. Somehow she had ignored her condition; because Guadalupe did not complain, Maria had not noticed how poorly she looked. "Thank you for reminding me, and I will attend to her as you say."

Carlos returned and stepped up to the wagon to stand smiling with Elena, both waving. In turn, Maria felt as if she and her mother were taking leave of family members. She now felt embarrassment at the contradiction between the anger she had been living with and the goodness shown by the couple. The hard anger was giving way to natural kindness and created a mixture of wonder and understanding.

19

Casas Grandes

Beyond this point, I had no more dreams for a time. Then late one night, the dreaming returned though in small scenes. Then larger segments of Maria's life emerged, one from just before her arrival in Casas Grandes. Maria confided in her mother that her menstrual periods had stopped. She was not sure what this meant, whether she was sick or was about to die. Guadalupe knew what was happening but sought to quiet Maria's fears by listening rather than explaining. She already knew, however, that Maria was pregnant from the rape from words that had come to her when she had prepared her husband and son for burial and from a dream she had had on the road.

Before reaching Elena and Carlos' home, Guadalupe had felt deeply feverish, made worse by the constant swaying of the wagon. It was then, as the fever worsened that Guadalupe entered a strange place of dreaming that foretold a miraculous birth. At first she said nothing to Maria for fear of again arousing her daughter's anger. Later, when unable to contain her excitement, Guadalupe quietly told Maria about the dream and what was to happen.

Maria's reaction was not what her mother expected. There was no anger. Instead Maria nodded as if accepting that her mother had been feverish as Elena had foretold. The improbable dream had to be a part of her fever.

Maria had other concerns. Since leaving the couple, she had begun to fully realize that she was responsible for her mother's life. The recognition was thrust upon her because of what Elena had said about her mother's poor health. Her mother had lost weight and so much more. Recognizing this, Maria suddenly felt tears falling.

Moments later she regained her composure and continued talking to herself. "Now I cannot forget what we must do … I'll watch mother, then before too long, as Carlos said, we should reach Casas Grandes."

Maria was correct. Soon they passed the small villages of Carretas, Janos, and Fronteras that Carlos had described, and finally they arrived at the outskirts of Casas Grandes. It was almost dark and lights flickered on in scattered adobe houses. Before going further, Maria stopped by a deserted road stand for a brief pause, helping her mother off the wagon.

It was late when they resumed the trip into town, and so Maria decided to wait to search for Guadalupe's sister in early morning. Quietly she stationed the wagon under the lamplights of the big plaza and went to buy food using the little money they had left. Soon Maria returned with cooked food and fed her mother and herself. Shortly, she led Guadalupe to her little corner in the back of the wagon. After making her comfortable, she lay next to her mother and both fell asleep.

Maria awoke to find a town much larger and busier than she had expected. The plaza was large. A huge church faced the square and government buildings lined another side. Stores and shops crowded the other two sides of the square, and everywhere people were meeting, talking, buying food and wares, and looking at the wagon standing off to the side of the road.

Maria quickly realized she had to move off of the square, and so she began to lead the wagon off into the side streets. Soon the big houses of the wealthy began to appear followed by the smaller adobe houses of ordinary people. As she looked, Maria thought, "I will be walking these streets with the big houses, and I'll find work. But first I must find my mother's sister who lives here, somewhere."

Maria expected that the sister, Esther, would welcome them and provide breakfast. She hoped Esther would allow them some shelter until Maria could find work and they could rent their own place. First, though, they had to find her.

As Maria led the wagon over many roadways asking for Esther's house, her mother continued her deep sleep. Unknown to Maria, Guadalupe had slipped into a coma brought on by her fever and the long nights of sleeping in the cold. Guadalupe was near death and nothing could save her.

20

Esther's House

From this point forward, I learned little more of Guadalupe except for her death and burial. I can only interpret what may have happened from sensing Maria's thoughts about Esther's house.

The search for Esther's house took hours. Finally, a kind neighbor led them to the house, explaining that this woman was not seen warmly by her neighbors. She was, said the neighbor, very quarrelsome and kept to herself in all ways. The woman's words caused fear in Maria, especially as she sensed the need for quick care for her mother and a place to stay.

Earlier Maria had stopped to look after Guadalupe and was frightened to see her condition. She hurried the mules along, wanting to arrive at the sister's house as soon as possible.

Esther lived in a small adobe house with a lean–to attached and a covered water well with a rope and bucket. The neighbor pointed to the lean–to. "Perhaps the sister will want you to place the wagon next to it, away from the street. She is very particular about wagons standing in front of her house." The neighbor left, not waiting to have further words with Maria.

Maria stationed the wagon and quickly turned to attend to her mother who lay curled in a fetal position. She climbed onto the wagon and cradled her head in the worn *reboso*. "Mother, we have arrived at the house and are waiting for your sister. She's gone, and we don't know when she'll be back. But just stay still, and I will get you some water." Maria hurried off to get water from the well and soon returned with a gourd dipper and helped her mother to drink. "You rest and I will find some food out in the street."

Later as Maria was feeding her mother, Esther returned from her work and found the two waiting for her. Instantly she became furious. It was unclear whether her anger was due to old grievances with Guadalupe or because they had arrived unannounced. She may have also feared that the neighbors had seen the two disheveled people sitting like vagabonds in her yard. Esther screamed that this would lower her status in the eyes of her neighbors.

Shortly Maria and Esther quarreled, but Esther said they could stay that night in a small storeroom. Later that same night, Guadalupe became extremely sick and by morning she died. Maria blamed Esther for her death because of the harsh words exchanged by the two. She decided to sell the mules and wagons and with the money rent a room. She managed a quick sale and left to rent lodging. Maria only approached Esther for help in arranging Guadalupe's burial in the local paupers cemetery. However, Esther refused to have her sister buried in a pauper's grave without a religious ceremony. So, instead, Guadalupe was buried in a cemetery of Esther's choosing, with proper religious ceremony.

Maria, meanwhile, quickly rented a room and began looking for work. Still, with her mother gone, she was confused and unsure of where to go or what to do. Furthermore, Maria now knew she was pregnant and increasingly feared what she was carrying in her stomach. And the nightmares were returning!

21

Father Eduardo

A dream fragment followed after the burial of Guadalupe. It involved Maria's meeting with a kindly priest and her search for an abortion as an end to the horror she imagined she was carrying.

Maria walked hurriedly past a small neighborhood church. It was evening and services had just completed. Because it was unusually warm, the church's sacristy door was open to the street. Maria innocently approached an elderly man wearing a white collar who was placing a clerical robe on a rack. Sensing her anxiety, he quickly asked her what the problem was. This was the beginning of her deep friendship with Father Eduardo.

In tears, Maria spoke of the recent death of her mother and of their long journey to get to Casas Grandes following the attack on her village. Father Eduardo especially listened closely since he had lost his mother just weeks before and was still grieving his mother's death when he heard Maria's story. Upon learning that Maria would live alone, he offered her a place with his housekeeper until she found domestic work. The housekeeper could look after her until the child came. Maria accepted his offer and soon was living in an attached house next to the priest's quarters with the old housekeeper, Angelina, with whom she quickly bonded. Angelina promised to assist her with the birth of the child when it came.

Soon, however, the nightmares began despite the warmth of her surroundings. Maria dreamed, too, of her mother's care, which she had not fully appreciated but now deeply missed. Through talks with Father Eduardo, Maria returned to dreaming of the love of her mother. In the dreams, she sometimes heard someone speak of the coming child.

In a moment known only by you, a woman,
you will feel new life in your body. It will bring
wonder about that child within, and
there will be no resistance or anger.

In that moment, you will reach back
to that instant in your child's mind,
to the wonder of seeing your first newborn infant.
Now a child is in you. The wonder is joyful!

Angelina spoke comforting words about Maria's coming baby, but she still felt confused and alone in the darkness of her small room.

As the baby in Maria's stomach grew larger, Guadalupe entered the dark room to lay with Maria and speak to her in Yaqui. She repeated softly the sentiments she had learned from her own mother.

When I knew you were to come,
it was the largest happiness I ever had.
And this happiness returned
with each child's coming. Time did
not matter then, it did not matter to grow old ...

Now, my daughter, you are to be in a world more real
than you imagined as a child. Then, you
dreamed of reaching into everyone's world, into
everyone's loving. Now you give and have the love of a child.

I will await and know of your joy.

That night Maria, hearing her mother's words in the throes of a nightmare, cried out, twisting her body in the darkness, searching for a reality.

Maria cried out softly. "My mother, let me know who I am now—how as a woman's body with child I can have joy with pain that is happening to me."

Maria fell asleep still crying and dreamed.

> A far off unraveling of long pieces of time
> from a huge ball of scratchy hemp. She saw herself
> unraveling more, more pieces and felt the wanting of a child
> seeking warmth. It lay among threads of her mother's
> soft hair, like that of village women she had watched and touched.
> There was softness in the tresses, black colors mingling
> with grays in wan memories, more strands pressing
> their textures and impressions on each remembrance
> of the mother's coming to the child's dream.
> And Maria dreamed that the strands were as a cord
> between each mother and child reaching
> an unseen distance, binding women figures she had known,
> all with warm faces of mothers holding children
> to their breasts.

> An insistent voice in Maria's dream was calmly saying,
> "Yet I ask you to take your ear from the earth and leave its pulse,
> move out of the sun, give up nights of warmth
> to keep their cold, so as to not forget your pain."
> And so softly that it could be a wind whisper,
> "Believe that you no longer believe.
> Give up wanting to share with others
> why loss of faith is so. Do not desecrate the corpses.
> Remain to wash them clean with me."

The strange voice faded, and the dream continued. Maria's unborn child sought to lead her by the hand, moving toward light. Maria resisted.

"I cannot leave the dead without an angry keeper. My dead is my flesh, as it is theirs. I cannot leave."

The dream became darker. "Were there time, and there is none now, or mother to hear me or father to speak to. Each is dead. I feel hurt and pain." Maria's nightmares continued.

22

Maria's Torments

In the nights that followed that dream, Maria's fears intensified. With her mother dead, she had no one to turn to for counsel or comfort except Father Eduardo. Her domestic work for a rich Mexican family provided food and bare necessities. However, Maria also suffered indignities and degradation and felt constant anger while she was there. Her fear of the coming birth was also mounting. And she could not forget what had happened to her family and home.

Earlier Maria had told Father Eduardo what had happened, including the rape. Now, in the midst of nightmares and fears regarding her evil fetus, she turned to him for help.

Increasingly the old priest's relationship with Maria deepened. He sensed that she was becoming a devout daughter of the church, and Maria moved him deeply as both a growing woman and an innocent child in need of worldly knowledge. However, he was horrified when Maria innocently turned to him for help locating a medical person to rid her of the fetus.

"My child, do you know what you are asking of me? Do you know of my vows as a priest?" Father Eduardo was speechless. He rose and paced before Maria in agitation. "I have taken a vow before God to support life and not to take it or to help someone to take it!" He walked out of the sacristy in anger, leaving Maria crying.

Maria was taken aback by his response, having placed her trust in him. She had only asked for help from the one she felt closest to after her mother's death. Maria knew nothing of priestly vows. She had been brought up with Yaqui gods and beliefs. On hearing the utter rejection of her plea for help, Maria cried and cried. Yet even through her tears, she knew that, somehow, she had to end the life growing within her if the nightmares were to end.

Father Eduardo returned, sat as before, and held her hand. "What I said before caused you alarm. You did not know anything of my church vows and so you innocently asked for help. And I should have explained my answer more gently. So now I'll say more." The priest hesitated, walked about, and then sat down.

"My daughter," he began, "you are feeling the first moments of knowing you will have a child." He paused, looking off. "Now, I am not a woman and do not know, but I recognize these as moments when a woman is most close to God. That is, when she chooses to give her love and caring to a child that comes to her body."

Maria, seeming not to understand, interrupted him. "But how can I have a child without a husband?"

The old priest, nodding as she spoke, answered quickly, "It is not a matter of having a husband. Rather, when you were violated, those men left their seed in you, and though that seed was from an act of violence, God turned it into a seed for goodness."

Father Eduardo could see that his words confused her. It showed in Maria's face, and he sought to help her comprehend. "Though you may find it difficult to understand, you have been chosen to receive a gift from God through that seed!"

Maria withdrew her hand from his and remained still for minutes, her face a cold mask. Then she rose and without speaking, quietly left his study. Father Eduardo watched her leave. At first, he thought of accompanying her, then he thought better of it. She would think on his words and would return to seek further counsel.

Maria reached the street feeling confused and angry. She knew for certain that she could not continue to live with the evil thing that caused her nightmares. "He does not understand … It is not a good thing that I carry. I will not continue living with this evil thing." If the old priest would not help her, she would find someone else. If she had to, she would spend the little she had saved from her work and what was left from the mules to find someone who would help.

Maria's steps quickened in anger. She remembered the man who sold herbs and potions. Earlier Maria had heard whispers of his powers to heal sickness and treat diseases. Through the priest's housekeeper—a good but unlearned woman—Maria also heard that some people feared him. She said that he could heal but could also put spells on the people he quarreled with. Father Eduardo did not trust him, she said, but he also knew that poor people needed the *curandero's* help with herbs.

As she walked, Maria considered whether she should find this man and if he would help rid her of the evil she was carrying. He would not harm her, especially if she paid him. Maria decided, she would find this *curandero* and ask for his help.

23

Hernan the *Curandero*

He wore
a faded homespun cap,
a beaked nose, brown black eyes,
and a face of ancient leather
with lineage to an ancient world.

He had crossed the wide dream
carrying herbal magic
and waited, patient.
I asked for a direction home.

He said there was none. I was home.
Then he continued on his path.

From the moment Maria decided to seek the *curandero's* help she thought of nothing else. She searched constantly for the old man at the market stalls and finally found him. Maria was deeply drawn to Don Hernan's power with herbs and potions, which increasingly seemed magical. In her naivety, she also dimly feared that his knowledge and power could harm her.

Still, the night after the first day they met, Maria's lingering nightmare lifted. She thought it was because of her expectation that he could help her. Her nightmare was replaced by a long dream filled with bits of images connected to the magical powers of Don Hernan.

> **In a dark place of a long dream, Maria waited,**
> **especially fearful of the spirits that were hidden**
> **in the mysterious rows of dangling herb pouches**
> **carried by the *curandero*. She heard of stories**
> **coming with the herbs and potions—especially from**
> **the potions he carried in mysterious inner pockets.**
> **The pockets were said to have even darker sides**
> **to them, and these sides, people said, had**
> **miraculous healing powers. They created great**
> **hope and helping reality to the user. The stories,**
> **herbs, and mysterious potions were for helping and**
> **healing and not for evil. Still, though Maria strangely**
> **perceived the fearful spirits, she was not**
> **drawn to their dark sides. And, no matter, said**
> **the dream, she could fully believe that Don Hernan**
> **would help rid her of the evil she was carrying.**

The *curandero* sold his herbs and potions in surrounding towns and markets and was usually gone for days. During his first absence after their meeting, Maria feared that he would not return. When they finally met he again listened to her pleas for help. He had to rid her of her growing nightmare and what she called her inner stomach growth. Don Hernan had surmised her real need but had kept from telling her the truth. As her pleas grew more insistent, he somehow found a way to tell her what he thought.

"I told you before I will pay you, and now I want for you to tell me what this thing is in my stomach and to help me get rid of it," Maria said, as she reached down to touch her stomach. The waiting child stirred strangely. It moved as if coming awake in a furious struggle as if it recognized the intent of her words. It recoiled.

The *curandero* noted Maria's sudden movement and heard the fear beneath her words. He sensed that she wanted proof from him that what lay in her stomach was evil. Don Hernan felt that it was the time to talk to her. He gently told Maria of her coming child and tried to allay her fears. He sought a dark market stall that was unoccupied.

"Let us stop here," he said, pointing to a corner of the stall. "Now loosen your skirt and raise your blouse so that I can touch your stomach." He lay his gnarled, warm hand on her smooth skin.

"It is a child and it is asleep," he said, gently. The child within responded to the warm hand and settled back peacefully. "It must be beautiful and gentle because it is at peace and asleep." He cooed the words. A gentle man by nature, Don Hernan acted in simple ways, using simple language. He acted from old intuition that went beyond his knowledge of herbs, potions, and plants.

In touching Maria's stomach, he suddenly felt fear that the child in this woman's body might be harmed. His fear coupled with the joy of feeling close to the child. He asked himself how he could tell this woman that the child was not the evil she imagined!

Maria waited. The old man's hand remained on her stomach, its touch mixing energy that meshed warm and strong at the base of his neck. Slowly, he removed his hand, continuing to feel the magical transformation that had come from the unseen person. Don Hernan had never been allowed this experience before. He had been told that it existed. Now he had direct knowledge.

The old man remained transfixed, continuing to feel the deepest tranquility in touching the unborn child that lay just below the surface of Maria's skin. Maria, meanwhile, was angry that he did not speak. She busily readjusted her blouse over her ungainly skirt.

"Tell me what you know!" she demanded. When he remained silent, Maria knew he would not share his knowledge. She demanded help, and when he only stood there, she began to cry. Her voice softened and then wailed as Maria pleaded for herbs that would put the child to sleep instead of being born. The old man knew he had to speak.

"Maria, I want you to know and to rejoice that you are to receive a special gift in the child you carry. Like you, I too am part of a Yaqui Mother, and I know and believe the gift is from *Nakawe, our grandmother who comes—a goddess of light.*" As he spoke, his gentle smile returned.

It came from his discovery of the child's touch, which felt like a revelation.

Maria was unmoved. The smile on the old man's face angered her. "So, old man, you will not help ... then I will find someone who can!" With utter coldness, Maria turned her back on the old man and dismissed him. She left him standing there. Perplexed, she did not understand or rejoice.

Slowly, he picked up his sacks of plants and clusters of bags and moved out into the activity of the town. He walked out slowly, sorrowfully. In his more than eighty years, he had never experienced the joy of touching a gift from *Nakawe*.

He walked hunched over as if awaiting a burdened fate like child hearing harsh arguments he does not understand. He had abandoned the child. For all his wisdom, Don Hernan could not intercede for good against the willfulness of rage.

**After the womb, where do life histories begin and what
accounts for their particular colorations and events?
There is much in each life, in each span between
being born and dying. And, oftentimes, there is
more notice of dying, through its achievements
and experiences, perhaps legacies, than often marks birth.
A few lives are celebrated when they begin.
More when they end.
It was not surprising then that beyond
the fear of her coming, Teresa's life
was first celebrated by a sorrowing man named Hernan.**

24

Maria's Nightmare and a Message

I, the observer, sensed professionally that Maria was becoming mentally unstable, perhaps mad, in the dreams I was receiving. Her emotional life lacked cohesion and reasoning. There were other indicators but none that clearly showed whether the deteriorating progression of her mind sprang from aspects in her childhood. More likely, her mental deterioration was related to the recent brutal circumstances in her life. She had lost her home, her family, had been brutally raped, and now found herself adrift without a home. And Maria thought she was now carrying an evil omen left by her attackers. She believed it was evil despite what the *curandero* said. I could feel her deep despair.

After Maria's final meeting with Don Hernan, she returned to her room saddened and without hope, unsure of what to do. She thought about destroying herself as a way to destroy the evil. She thought too of thrusting a knife into her stomach to end the life of whatever was there. If she did, she somehow expected that she would survive.

That first night after meeting with Don Hernan, Maria fell asleep without eating, lost in despairing thoughts. The old nightmares that pursued her returned and continued into the coming nights.

Crazed demons—visions shared and traded with
childhood friends, ghosts of unknown life, monstrous
dreams of children—settled easily, fearfully,
passing nearby and distantly in Maria's sleeping mind.
Childhood hurts returned as she slept.
Maria moved into a shell-like place, toward a
deepening sleep, passing over physical pain. Scenes
of recent deaths came from the left side of
her vision one by slowing one. Then all was peaceful;
in the silence of the shell-like place, she was being
handed ... a gift ... a small seed, like a grain
of golden yellow corn. Still, she drifted cloudlike
over the scene. The unknown hand held the gift and
offered it. The child stood separate, not accepting,
and the grain left the hand and floated about the
child form. And as the seed followed, it became a second
faceless child that later walked beside the first.

The motions of writhing demon figures remained mute,
watching as they and Maria looked on the featureless
children moving within their drifting state.
The dream world was silent.
Maria remained separate and still within the
soft and warm interior of lost sleep.
Then coming from within the dream began
insistent echoes, reaching far and back beyond
the fears of childhood. These came without remembering—
as separate echoing waves of voices once heard in the
world, upon the grasses, in visions of far mountains,
in the warmth of springs, and in the clouds of summers.
The thin rolling sounds linked in sounds of words.

As I observed, Maria's nightmare unfolded as my own dream, and I experienced it with her. The dream I observed finally formed itself into words that sounded as if they were a pronouncement, a message. And the words were spoken as by an old, patient voice: professorial, gentle, and soft yet carrying purpose.

**Wise persons understand that irony in life
is made from ordinary parts and that the results of this
are wondrous. That a child will pass through violence
upon its body and mind to gain a gift of life.
That a child can be spared to carry a seed that struggles
to blossom within her. And that before this happens,
a first test will occur. Life and madness will meet
to sense the other's force and to create separate triumphs.
A child's body in its fifteenth year will be the
place and time of this meeting. And the struggle
will be in unforeseen times of darkness, when
a grappling of life and death happens in unknown
ways within an unheralded, frail body—an ordinary
place of miracles.**

**The first test, then, is to know if an unwanted seed
survives a madness. And a second miracle is bound
within a second test. That if unwanted life survives ...
that it be a woman of light from which comes
the larger miracle that awaits a coming to pass.
From unwanted seed, then, is created a woman of very old
power, known since time of first creation ... always
coming anew in successive times, bringing gifts of
peace and goodness. She is called by one known voice.
She comes from the other side of violence, from a center
of peace, and she arises from the struggling center of
both to be in a call.**

From old time comes violence to change the center
of lives away from their generous natures. These are in
tests from which emerge tests of power. And from each
struggle in the center of life and death are left parts
of goodness. And these become as in the growing body
a call to goodness. And in the way of a miracle, there is
created a time and a coming of a new woman of Seataka!

She is for forever one of many. Each lives
a spiritual life within an outward reality of the world.
She is always in all human life and so then in all
lives and in ordinary times and frailties.
She serves from within ordinary precious natures. And
she comes to all lands, among all peoples, and to the
centers of all things. She will come to restore a
natural goodness from human arrogance and its violence.
She need only be a miracle to emerge herself a miracle.
And such a woman awaits ...

The voice spoke softly in receding echoes until it became a whisper
and died away.

25

Teresa's Birth and Her Beginning

Dear reader: this part of the story is mysterious and I as the observer accept it as so. It asks for your suspension of disbelief so as to accept its wonders and spirituality as coming from another place than we may know.

After nights of learning of the tragic parts Maria's life, I discovered a new life: Teresa. Thereafter, Teresa's life unfolded gradually until her own death. I saw her birth, her early life with Father Eduardo, and her harsh childhood of indentured service in a church workhouse. Later, she spoke of family life in Chicago as an immigrant woman. Then gently, Teresa prepared for her death in the company of her wounded son in the southwest. Throughout, Teresa's life was spent in celebration.

Before I came to know Teresa, there was a long period of calmness where I did not dream of Maria or her life. It was as if Maria was lost after her constant presence in my dreams and sometimes in my daytime moments. Her absence lasted for days, then weeks.

Finally, Teresa's voice and first words came to me from somewhere, soft and gentle. She spoke of remembering her birth as a prelude to the telling of her life. There began my knowledge about this wondrous woman, a knowing one. She spoke as if in conversation.

Once in a far time, there was a reality to what
I tell you now. Accept the dream, and you will understand
it as a story, a tale. Yet hear the words as shadows of
things that happened, like the sun that moves across
tall trees leaving lines of insubstantial form.
The words stay, and shadows leave the world where we
walk, and things are touchable.
Leave then to be in timelessness and inside and
outside of ourselves; be sure, and yet go
without direction that we can know.

My words are made in the dream place of the mind,
making things remembered different from when they began.
It is as sleep is different from the dream, and
things are only what they are said to be.
For I remember that, as a baby, when you cried
your sound was heard and my feeling was felt. And when
I dreamed it, words were no longer binding tight
what the words meant. Still, I am sure my baby
cried and I am sure of the dream.

So, the tale I tell has ordinary things and shadows,
and I have returned a long way to be with you.
So I once again rely on a small assistance from you ...
to guide me since I have little intuition here
in our touchable reality. Here, I seem to trust less
and fear more, and I hear that acceptances come measured
and have lost openness. And words are used in many ways
as "love" so very often is. Their meaning is confusing,
as when my brother acts against his nature and
kills for love of things and a place called "country"
and my sisters sometimes praise his violent acts.
So I remained elsewhere with my sadness.
Now I return to you and this land of remembered home
where I see such goodness in this land of pain.
And here my tale of reality begins.

Here Teresa's voice softened almost to a whisper, and her words became more cadenced as if she were reaching into memory for what she sought to express.

I can begin by saying that we each know when
life begins for us. Then we know when intuition gives us
knowledge of light, movement, comfort, feelings that
surround a one called mother who nurtures and carries us
for much time in that different life. And that time is the
closest that we can ever be to another; that is as close
as we are to ourselves.

Experience begins there,
formed from a much earlier intuition. And experience
moves from feeling to piecing and storing
of experience. Then we are in a first world of knowing,
with a first knowledge that is slowly lost by many.
It is intuition and perception without learning,
obscured by reality.

Then we are sure in knowing that our being, the
center of mind, begins within a mother's own being and mind
held in her whole body that is passed to the child.
Together, then, the centers begin the first beating
of the child's heart in rhythm and manner unknown to each
yet following unspoken teachings of Ometeotl,
a supreme creator—an omnipotent, omniscient one.

Soon, calmness is natural to the carried and the carrier,
like parts together elsewhere in sky over earth,
sun, and moon, and stars, as ocean water and fish.
And that which continues to happen is *Seataka*,
a divine gift, as is faith.

And both lives continue, being and becoming
as both move through the child heart. Sound,
light, fluid, nurturing reach again and again
through both beings, and in a time, limbs begin to move, adjust.
Voices speak somewhere, faintish light appears past a
thin, whitish wall. Images appear through eyes closed and seeing.
Eyes see as in a dream, and feelings change
to peacefulness or stir anxious—or fear comes hurtful
with noise or angry movements.
Emotions from afar filter through to easy and uneasy
sensing and remembering.
The beings are each experiencing new life.
Neither feels or acts alone or remembers alone.
Still, each is different, together.

In this first dream, I sensed Teresa speak as if the message I was hearing was for her mother, Maria. I felt like an eavesdropper. Still, I shall share what followed.

I dreamed once when you were first new to me
that I was inside then outside of myself,
being, saying words from both places. Then I awoke
and learned your being was always with me.
If I felt, you were feeling; where I turned to see and hear,
you would turn, see, and hear. That is when I knew of
love and loving, that of *Seataka*, and then I knew
of coming pain. It was not of birth but of living.
I was to know the sadness of people—that having been
together in all ways with another, they still destroyed
the body from which they came where they had known
love and peace. If evil appeared this way, from such roots,
what could not be destroyed?
Best I turn away to life and being born.

Then feeling continues, moves toward and from each being
through fluid walls of gentleness and resistance ...
through places where each press toward and away from the other.
This happens as each has larger and larger size
and a curiosity, each for the other, about their existence.

Thoughts of each are as premonitions and shadows to the other—
distant, remote. They are strangers and friends that have never
met, as some daughters and mothers will later be so in
another life. Yet, each clings to the other, now
sharing sleeping and awake dreams, their lives, and all moments.

The inner life seeks images, voices beyond the thinning wall,
unfamiliar lights, and listens when the other sleeps.
The mother feels movements, changes of place,
knows inside times of sleeping and fear
and creates holding and sounds of comfort.

And in one moment, in a new time for each being,
the two are filled with divine surety and faithfulness.
One life prepares to leave semidarkness in journey.
The other wills it and aids it to be so.

After a time, Teresa's voice stopped sounding soft as if in conversation and moved quietly into a rhythmic cadence. It pulsed gently with a power of excitement.

It is thus that I remember my birth. When sounds were
louder, different than before. There were heavy falling movements.
The feeling was of changing light and darkness.

I lay in warm peace. It was still a dark part of time.
My mother's body was calmer than it had been.
Few movements were between us; it was soundless sleep.

Slowly and suddenly I awoke to a pounding and strong heat,
to the straining of limbs against a body.
I remember fear coming in stronger and stronger rhythms
and choking pressures and beginning to move
through dark places where I could not hold or stay.
Pressure quieted and returned, pushing, pulling
toward a deepness that held for a long, long time.

Then fear became sound in everything, and then
fear was gone. New sound filled all space and senses and
had a light within it that was as one with tranquility.
That sound was as wind would later be on the hills
and mountain tops and in grassy plains—rushing, rolling
with strength as it moved. And the light in the sound
slowly took shape and color, glistening like sun on water.
Sound and light grew, filled all being and place.
And I was born in that light and sound.

And then, suddenly, the excitement that had been rising in Teresa's voice dropped away, subdued.

Something had happened, and her voice gained a sorrowing quality.

In moments as well, I remember awakening to cold.
About me there is darkness again, now without peacefulness.
Surfaces cause pain. I am cold from a cold hand touching.
Then a warm hand replaces the cold one, gripping one.

Voices rise, angry. I am brusquely placed in roughness
and cold. The sound and light are gone.
Someone cries and is angry.
That was at the moment of birth, when tranquility
and pain came together.

Later when I awoke, I could not know that I had
all the senses I needed to live in the world.
I remember knowing about touch, its feeling. I could
see shapes and lights. I had simple knowledge like
a small animal. I also sensed hurt and anger from another
and knew a difference from the earlier peace.

And I had come to the pain of uncaring. My mother, I learned
later, would not hold me. She had learned of my coming
from a man of herbs, a *yuemhitebia*. He told her
that I would work with people to nurture goodness and that
I would thus have human power that she would come to
understand
and to help me gain. She chose to not understand.
Later, I would learn in my growing that my angry mother
feared what she sheltered and would not disarm her rage.
She would ignore me, but later, my intuition would
remove that. Later she would beat and hurt the child.
I came to understand. And with nothing left to take,
she withdrew herself, she removed my mother.

26

Teresa's Life

In the course of knowing about Maria, Teresa, and the family's tragedy, I learned about the history of Mexico and its national life. Thereby, I came to understand the context in which they lived and died and the obstacles they faced. In particular, I learned of events faced by Teresa that were different from those facing Maria.

The events of Teresa's life after her birth in 1908 were a mystery because the nature of the dreams I had experienced up until then changed. Where before I had fully known the feelings and observed the behaviors of participants, now I witnessed only bits of these. I experienced hints of Teresa's thoughts and actions. Later her grown and wounded son Juan also appeared in a dream to speak for her, but this happened infrequently.

It was as if, gradually, a veil or curtain of privacy had descended over Teresa's life and thereafter little became known. My dreaming almost stopped again. Having spent so much personal time enmeshed in the life of this family, I pondered this change. I asked myself, what could this change mean? Had the dreaming run its course? Was there nothing more to share? Had I, through an inadvertent or personal shortcoming, caused my release from their lives?

Then, quietly, almost surreptitiously, fragments of Teresa's thoughts began to reemerge. The first time when Teresa reemerged she began to speak very slowly. Her sporadic words led me to understand what was happening in her world.

A good priest and an old woman who tended his life
fed me, provided warmth in cold nights
that followed a first night.
Then without much else, my mother left for home,
somewhere, and I was left alone to grow.

If I stay close to old, old memory,
I still feel the old woman's caring sounds as she
brought our faces to the other. I hear sounds of her
words, the gentle look of eyes with tears,
cradling murmurs.

Then in that old way that I dimly remember, I remember
standing and walking, and then waiting for
the good man and old woman to return.
In time, in intuition time, I knew I was alone.
Then a tall man dressed all in black came
to take me by the hand into a new world called
a place of church work.

In the dreams that began to reemerge, Teresa was old and reliving her past life. Instead of viewing her story as if experiencing it in the present, I saw only parts of what had happened to Teresa. And through the means of these limited dreams I learned the manner of *Seataka* in creating a Woman of Power.

As Teresa grew into womanhood, she did not exalt in the power that she possessed. That power was always anonymous. A woman of *Seataka* is not vainglorious. She simply used her power to affect people's lives in good ways. It was as if she had no other choice.

Teresa and I had an unspoken pact that I did not need to know of the times she affected lives for good. To disclose this power to an observer would violate the trust placed in her by *Seataka*.

I understood this as the reason for the change in the content of the dreams I witnessed. I accepted this limitation and, perhaps, thereby maintained access to the important events in Teresa's life. In the coming pages, I narrate my interpretations of Teresa's story rather than direct observations.

Teresa remembered being placed in a church workhouse at about age three. Earlier, she had been nurtured by the priest's aged housekeeper, but the housekeeper became ill and could no longer care for her. Rather than placing her in an orphanage, she and the priest both believed that the workhouse would provide religious instruction and domestic training to enable Teresa to enter into a good marriage.

Ultimately the workhouse provided only hard work and drudgery. The placement happened just prior to the Mexican Revolution whose goals included the destruction of the Catholic Church, its structure, and priesthood. This affected Teresa's life in several ways.

In an early dream in which Teresa described her placement, she spoke of the many indentured children—all females—placed in the workhouse who were cared for, punished, and controlled by older girls.

Every day, they awoke in darkness to eat a gruel made of corn and cold corn tortillas before they set off to work. They milled corn, kneaded flour, made tortillas, washed clothes, scrubbed stone floors, and ironed religious frocks. Many of the things they made, washed, and ironed were ordered and paid for by wealthy parish families. When she described these times, Teresa mostly spoke easily without rancor or anger. At times, she even remembered moments of humor.

**We managed to live, the most of us that did not become sick,
until men called Villistas or Carranzistas came.
We did not know which, but I do remember we were alone.
The priests and sisters had all left.
And then we sat on long benches.
Then the men came and took the oldest and prettiest ones.
The small ones like us were left behind.**

We were too little; nobody wanted us.

**Later we spoke among ourselves, asking each other,
"And who are your parents?"**

I remember this little one, so serious,
she answered, "Why I do not know," and thinking again
said solemnly, "I know—I think I am an *hija de la tierra!*"
"A child of the earth!" and then I remember
laughing, thinking, "Well I am too, I am like that!"

And later an old woman and an old man
looked after us, and I cared for the children too.

This little one, especially.
She had one leg shorter than the other and
she hobbled when she walked. We were together much
of the time because she worried and was sad and serious,
always wondering about her parents.
She would ask about mine. I thought I had parents
but most of the others thought they had none. So
after a while, I began to say I did not know mine.
And it was true inside of me to know that
my parents were strangers, and like the other children,
I did not have parents. Those words satisfied the children.
Afterwards, they spoke of themselves as children of the earth.
The earth was like parents, and it was
important to be with something.

The Mexican Revolution went on for years, but Teresa remembered that the revolutionaries never returned for young women. Teresa had been spared to care for the many cold, sick, hungry children in the workhouse. She spoke of burrowing among them on their thin mattresses of straw and ticking to share long cold nights. When the children quarreled, Teresa settled arguments and helped them resume friendships. She remembered that the older, bigger girls tried to be in charge of everything and did not like to have a smaller girl—Teresa—settle arguments.

The big girls would have preferred that the children argue and fight so they could beat them. Often, Teresa settled the arguments and endured beatings for problem children. It was a way, Teresa recalled, of caring for the smallest, more helpless ones who were often the victims. Teresa also recalled much earlier times when men in black coats and sisters in white hats still lived on the church grounds.

Once when she was six or so years old, she wanted to look closely at the tall figure hanging on what seemed to be white sticks. His body was almost without clothes, and it had a hole on the chest with blood on it.

> **Early Sundays in darkness before regular people came,**
> **we had to pray in a big church next to the workhouse.**
> **It was cold—we never had warm clothes—but always**
> **there was warmth and light coming from candles placed**
> **under the figure standing without clothes.**
> **Always, I thought the candles were to keep him warm.**
>
> **I was a child. I watched him many times wanting to know**
> **if he was sleeping or paining from**
> **the cut and blood on his side.**
>
> **One morning, I stayed behind in the darkness**
> **and climbed up to touch the man. When I touched**
> **him, the figure's feet and legs were cold. They**
> **felt of stone as the cold stone floor I scrubbed almost**
> **every day. No one saw me.**
> **I climbed down, knowing it was just all stone.**

Teresa only knew life in the workhouse until she was about twelve. During that time, an old priest who no longer wore a frock or collar returned to look after the workhouse. Quietly, he took charge of matters that had been left in the hands of the older girls, some of whom remained unmarried and were unwilling to give up their power. Under his gentle direction, things returned to what they had been—almost without harsh punishments!

When Teresa was nearing age thirteen, she was allowed to leave the workhouse to arrange for work with the remaining wealthy families and to deliver laundry and foodstuffs prepared by the girls. She found a whole new world to explore: big homes and families with people who loved one another. It was another world!

Teresa sensed many things about the families as she spoke to the maids, the gardeners, and others. Slowly, she began to understand that most grown people were not much different from the children she had grown up with. She learned that they fought, became jealous, had resentments, and mostly hid what they felt until they found ways to show their feelings in hurtful ways. Then she met Francisco, a young son of one of the wealthy families that she sometimes worked for.

Francisco was about fifteen years older than Teresa, and she heard he was a world traveler. He and his brother ran a growing business making *rebosos,* shawls traditionally worn by Mexican women. He was the traveling salesman for the business, which took him to Mexican cities to the north and into the border cities of the United States.

In time, Teresa became a live-in housemaid and found opportunities to speak with Francisco. From the beginning, she found him the most handsome, interesting man she had ever known, though as Teresa admitted later, she knew few men. Still, she found him a gentleman who never took advantage of his social position. Their friendship grew, and after a time, he asked to marry her.

Teresa was excited and also confused. She wanted to marry Francisco, but she also knew that the family would object to his marrying an orphan girl of uncertain parentage. But Francisco was a freethinker, and he was able to contradict the family's demands and even religious beliefs. He thought little of religion and wanted only to have a civil marriage ceremony.

Ultimately, Teresa agreed to marry Francisco in a civil service. However, in retribution his family ordered him to leave the city and end his business dealings with his brother. Francisco had to sell his share of the business to his brother. With the money he made, he decided to take his bride to Chicago. He had heard much about that city, and he wanted to live there. He was also sure he would easily find work to support them.

Teresa felt both happy and sad about the move. She related deep feelings about the separation from her friends in the workhouse, many whom she had known from early childhood. Though Teresa had begun to work and live away from the workhouse, she always visited the children on her free time. Leaving them after a visit was difficult, but suddenly she realized that she would be gone from them for a long time, possibly forever. It was difficult to accept.

Almost as if I were a young, innocent child
I wanted to stay with my sisters, feeling they
were my daughters, and I their mother.
And it could not be so. Still,
I remember aching, and it was as if
I was first learning about crying.

Now I recall, many were always sick.
I think some died, and I helped a few.
We all just tried to avoid being punished,
to eat, to just live. And I think
that there was too little time left to love one another.
There was little time left from our work and survival.
I remember, sadly, we learned so little of religion.

There seemed to be little time left, even for God.

27

Teresa's Later Life

As I noted earlier, after some time the dreams about Maria and her family changed. I thought that they had ended. Still, I expected that in time, I would learn something more of their lives. And I was rewarded: the messages resumed, though only in the words shared by Teresa. These messages were no longer visual; I was hearing but no longer seeing what was described. My role then was to accept and interpret an account of what she shared, and this I did faithfully.

After marrying and before leaving for the United States, Teresa experienced her first vision while in the village in Baja. Subsequently, she underwent her transformation as a woman of *Seataka* that she recounted in an earlier dream. It was there, too, that she learned from her own dreams that in the near future she would be a mother herself. She was overjoyed, but she did not tell Francisco at that time. Teresa wondered how the birth could happen in light of their pending trip north. She was concerned but was certain all things would be resolved. The resolution did happen, but under unexpected circumstances.

After a delay in their hometown, Francisco and Teresa were ready to leave for Baja, California. After their visit in Baja, there was another delay in finding transportation north into the United States. The delays worried Francisco; their funds were being depleted, and he was not working. So upon reaching Topeka, Kansas, he sought temporary work in the city's railroad yards. However, Francisco lacked winter clothing, and in the bitter cold of the Kansas winter, he caught pneumonia.

Fortunately the two had a room in the railroad's temporary housing, and Teresa was able to care for Francisco. He soon recovered but then had a serious relapse. Throughout this period, Teresa supplemented their dwindling savings by cooking and washing laundry for the railroad workers. Finally Francisco was able to work, but he had to take dangerous train wreck repair work, which involved absences from Teresa that lasted for days. Meanwhile Teresa awaited their first child.

28

The Birth of Luz

Teresa recounted feelings of loneliness, isolation, and fear of being alone in a small room barely heated or lighted as the birth drew near. Fortunately, she had become close friends with Marita, the wife of another railroad worker. Marita had experience as a midwife and had promised to be with Teresa upon the baby's birth. Still, Teresa knew that Marita had her own children to look after including a very young baby. So Teresa was concerned that her friend would not be able to help with the baby's birth. It worried Teresa more and more.

Teresa spoke to me repeatedly of her fear of being alone, a fear that seemed to come from her past life and her feelings of abandonment in the church workhouse.

> **I remember, then, feeling new responses in my body.**
> **And I remember crying out for Marita.**
> **Then I thought to just stay lying down**
> **to see if the feelings of pressure would pass.**
> **Later, my stomach felt painfully heavy,**
> **and the mind felt sick with fright.**
> **No, Marita had not heard my cries.**

As Teresa continued speaking, she sounded less frightened, less hysterical and became easier in her words and tone. Just as her mother had after the rape, Teresa was escaping the pain she was now reliving.

Teresa had fled, escaped into a time of tranquility. She had returned to a time in the workhouse and a place that, no matter what, had served as home.

Once when she was very young, Teresa was instructed to deliver clothes to a parish family. Unfamiliar with the streets, she had strayed from her intended destination and then, curious, decided to look into the home of an ordinary family to see what a family was like. After living her entire life in the workhouse, the concept was novel.

Teresa found herself in a very poor barrio. A wall of rooms faced the street. It was early summer, and the door was open to the first room she came to. Its threshold caught direct yellow light, its boundaries sharp as a knife's edge across the entrance. The light burned into the adobe floor scalloped by bare feet over many years. The room was a cubicle closed to sound by thick adobe walls and a hard dirt floor. Teresa called out; no one answered. She remembered feeling that home felt deserted, empty.

She wandered further. The door to the next room was closed, its doorframe scarred, old paint colors showing through chipped places. The doorways seemed like entrances to cells that should not have people in them. And the doorways all marched evenly across the low adobe wall, roofed over with old red tile, cracked in places. Vines and supporting wattle had broken through. Birds chirruped in the hollows added muted gaiety, contrasting with the sound of the hot noonday stillness. It was as if home was an empty place, with no one to be found.

Teresa's mind fled from the scene as if it offered nothing of what she imagined home to be. The workhouse at least had her friends.

Then I heard Teresa's words hesitate, and suddenly, she had returned to the room and to her sounds of strangled pain. She sounded fearful and alone.

**I remember returning from somewhere and
being in our small room again. I had brought back from
where I went a shaft of orange, yellow, golden light.**

**Now the light moved, sparkled with the hours. In the
windowless darkness it was a warm friend.**

> **I remember struggling to sit, then to move. Then**
> **I tried to reach past the smallish doorway to find Marita.**
> **The doorframe resisted my large body.**
> **I was crying, saying Marita promised to help, to**
> **be with the birth. I still hear my voice, calling**
> **again and again as old people do when no one listens.**
> **Then I reached the door to sink down**
> **against the wall. The cold wooden floor felt good;**
> **it kept me upright.**

Teresa's words came through heavy breathing. She spoke of sweat matting her hair, of her body becoming cold and then bursting hot. Nausea, she said, stayed like a fever. Images twisted through sounds, moments lived in the workhouse. Teresa began to speak with her inner child through the long, dark hours. She spoke softly, distantly, as if the sounds were murmured only to a child sleeping somewhere in her body.

> **We are as life companions, you and me.**
> **Where we go, we go together.**
> **I cannot leave you. I will dress and feed you,**
> **laugh with you and care for you and keep you.**
> **Stay. We cannot be alone again.**

Suddenly, I saw inside of Teresa's mind for the first time in many dreams. The sudden shift may have occurred because of her mixture of utter fear and peacefulness about her coming child.

What I now witnessed were images slipping through different realities. Teresa was touching the unborn child. Magically, she had arrived at the church workhouse and was describing the scene to the child.

> **There were long stone floors, cold and moist**
> **in first light. The stone shone as with rain,**
> **and it was cold to the bare feet. In dark mornings**

before a big bell rang, we woke to each other
from our warmth. We did not move too much as you do.
It was cold on stone floors, walking dark corridors
before real light. Moonlight did not enter. Girls
talked of evil things in that darkness and of the priest
of the church protecting us.

Teresa laughed softly in the eerie trance state, her pain lines softening.

I still ran through the darkness to the kitchen
and to the kitchen woman with the switch. I accepted
beatings before I accepted evil ghosts.
Know that I could not beat you. Loving you as myself
has removed a need to hurt others or to feel
intended pain placed by others.

Teresa smiled as if she knew the child surely understood her thoughts and words. Then she drifted further away and returned hours later, strangely saying, "Feeling each nerve has its own memory." Wonder showed through an occasional closing of her eyes. An image emerged in which Teresa suckled her child—only the child was Teresa. Then, quiet lay over the moments as Teresa readied herself to confront violence from her faintly remembered mother.

Teresa saw her mother holding many children, calmly moving as others assailed her with anger and shouting. She remembered living with a mother and father, with the priest and Angelina. Home was a mother wanted and then remembered, strong as the earth. And Teresa felt familial images, seen in a bar of light laying across a doorway.

Then Teresa again turned to the child she thought she was holding.

Know I will not hurt you as my mother did me.
She said I slept or cried little.
This brought weariness to my mother's outward actions.
When she acted dishonest, hurtful to others, my mother
felt I knew this or so it seemed to her.

And when she beat me because of this, I could only reply
by holding to my mother. I had less fear
because I understood her anger.
This may have been loving. This brought her fear
and a stronger evil. Know now that I do not fear you
as she did me. I will only love, keep, and care for you.

Childbirth pain returned to Teresa in her dark room. The bright light had left and evening was softer except for a mounting hurt. At that moment, she could not recall whether the fear that accompanied pain was for her or for the coming child.

Teresa kept repeating, "Marita, *por favor* … Marita!," and her cries rose as from a wounded animal. The crying echoed uncertainly and dropped, muffled and hidden from habit, bound in by years of obedience.

"Francisco," she cried out then realized he was gone, working somewhere. Teresa cried quietly, feeling the awkward protrusion of new life in hesitant movements. Her thin arms clutched her abdomen, the misplaced burden feeling heavy, unwieldy. Nausea came in waves with the exertion. The movements of the new life gathered strength and pushed in her stomach, struggling for light and air. There were small moments away from the pain.

Teresa said, "It is as the miracle of Mary with Jesus we learned in the instruction. And Mary had lived with her peaceful son until he was killed." Slowly with lessened pain, she was less frightened for herself and gave more strength and care to the coming life. Both beings rested in the darkness.

I remember now how daylight came into our gentle,
loving place. First light awakened the awkwardness.
It returned to carry away fear, faceless and terrible
as it had been in the body. Then my new child came forth,
called Luz—Light. The bond was set
even before Marita finally awoke and came
to sever the life cord.

29

Immigrants in Chicago

F inally bound for Chicago, Teresa was feeling stronger and was no longer afraid. Waves of enthusiasm and joy emerged in her dream while on the train trip. I sensed her growing power and the maturity of her role as a young mother, possessed of serenity, sureness, and renewed creative energy. Teresa retained a childlike curiosity, especially about her new world of Chicago.

At first, in the dream Teresa spoke in measured ways. Later, her words took on a conversational, almost storytelling tone. From past dreams, I also recognized Yomumuli, her mentor, speaking behind Teresa's words. She had been instructing Teresa about women leaving home. My dream seemed as if the two had been conversing earlier and their thoughts lingered. Yomumuli's words reached through in that dream Teresa shared with me.

**Beyond birth, humans renew to face death in all things
and to have change. Women know this first about their lives.
See and you will see. Women face life with grace,
gain strength, bend as strong trees, change, and grow.
Women are given and give love, and they give to
the seasons of others.**

**Women leave where they first grow and then spend
their whole lives building places for others**

and themselves to be with others in caring ways.
These places they mostly build alone, with few, few men,
and women create and then thread people into memories
and into families that, in loneliness, they fear having and
then love always. It is of the children carried alone,
spoken to alone in the wondrous moment of their coming,
and held alone until one or other dies—so there
lies the most gentle loving of women.

And it would be as if any woman is borne this
way in loving: children remain hers, whether of her body
or another's. The loving of life is always real within
a woman's heart. So it is that women make and keep their
own and those of others that are then lovingly taken by
death and nature ... and more so destroyed in the
violence and meanness of so many men.

And nothing will be likened to the gentle loving of women.
They keep the children and keep the memories
and hold others and keep the world.

Teresa continued in her own soft-spoken tone. She described how
she, Luz, and Francisco arrived in Chicago in the cold winter of 1920.
Her words were now in clearer English and contained expressions she
learned in Kansas. I added small interpretations to Teresa's words.

After a long trip on the train, we got
to the very big city called Chicago, and we had to go
a long way past many, many houses to get to the
very big place where all the people got off. It was
late at night and very cold, and there was wind with snow,
and we waited until a big car called a streetcar
came, and we got on. I was holding Luz and keeping her
as warm as I could. Before, Francisco had asked how to get
to his friend's house and the car to take.

**And so we began a ride on the car that was very
cold except it had a little warm air coming from down by the
walls of the car. We two and Luz were alone with the
driver who got out of the car many times to pull on a long
stick outside to get what was called a power line
to make the car go on. This happened often times, and the
man was angry, but he kept getting out.
After a long ride on the car, he stopped it and
told us how to get to the house where Francisco had a friend.**

When Francisco, Teresa, and the baby Luz arrived in Chicago, it was in the coldest part of winter. Francisco, "Pancho" as Teresa called him, had recovered, but he still worried about having enough money to last until he would be able to work. He was a strong, fairly large man who liked working with his hands as he had done on the railroad job in Kansas. He would look for railroad work in Chicago. Pancho had also learned some English, and he felt that would help him quickly find a job.

Chicago, however, offered few jobs. Following the first world war, immigrants crowded into the United States joining others that had arrived at the turn of the century. So by 1920, the city had many newcomers—mostly from Europe but some from Mexico, including those escaping the Mexican Revolution. The immigrants mostly came from farms and villages and were accustomed to manual labor. So Pancho faced competition.

Nevertheless, as soon as Francisco and Teresa settled in with their friend who also came from their hometown, Pancho set out to look for work every morning at the earliest hour. His determination and knowledge of English paid off. Within weeks, he was working as a laborer for the Pennsylvania Railroad along with men of all nationalities. Because he was respected and spoke some English, Pancho quickly rose to be foreman of a section gang working on train wrecks, the same work he had done in Kansas. Best of all, he was assigned housing in the railroad's work camp.

Thereafter, life was very good, especially after they began to have more children. A son, then another son was born, followed by two girls.

In time, Luz and the oldest son Juan were enrolled in a nearby public school, making Teresa and Pancho very proud. Teresa made friends with the wives of other workers living in the camp. After a time, she was able to leave the younger children in the care of other women, freeing her to explore the larger neighborhood. When possible, she explored everywhere with Luz, and slowly Teresa traveled further, finally going to Chicago's Loop by streetcar and train.

> **The camp was a safe place. The house in the camp
> was inside of two high roads where trains passed all the time. But
> after a while, I wanted to see more of things around there.
> So I took Luz to the park, some stores, and later to the Lake
> Michigan beach. From there, I saw faraway big houses
> standing like mountains. So later, I just had to go there.**

From that Lake Michigan beach, Teresa looked north and saw the far-off line of tall buildings she later learned was called the "Loop." Teresa later asked people at the stores how to get to the Loop. She got instructions and even had some people write the information down. After making many arrangements regarding care of her children and with Pancho's approval, Teresa took a streetcar, then a train, and finally arrived to look up at the big buildings. She was excited after that first visit when she spoke of it in her dream.

> **I felt unsure, not knowing all about English,
> but there was much to see so I forgot and watched everything.
> Many, many people moved all the time. The people
> talking, excited, looking at the tall buildings called
> skyscrapers, closing off light. I began to feel
> small, but people were nice, and when I asked for something,
> they smiled and listened and helped me to understand
> things if I asked. Later, I had to get back on the
> train first with people sitting and standing and some
> reading and everyone with good manners.**

Life was turning out well for Teresa and Pancho. Luz, almost ten, and Juan and the other children were getting good grades in school. As hard as settling in Chicago had been, their life was now in place and Teresa was finding more time to help others.

It was in that role of helping that Teresa began to recognize Luz as more than a daughter. Luz was growing insightful and was able to understand the struggles and the pain felt by couples living on very meager monies with the demands of growing children. She listened and, despite being so young, offered words of comfort. She slowly began to help very young mothers with their babies and to soothe their often-quarreling children. Teresa, watching these qualities unfold, again heard the words first echoed in the long ago vision. Then it had been said that, as a woman of power, Teresa would gravitate toward women with similar qualities. As she discovered these women, Teresa would nurture those qualities and, if it were to be so, Ometeotl, would see them as possible women of power. Luz, she felt, could be such a woman—she *would* be!

Wives in the camp especially needed help. Early on, Teresa began helping mothers enroll their children in kindergarten and taught them basic words they could use in shopping. Teachers welcomed her in their classrooms to translate for mothers. Teresa practiced her English and was able to help other immigrant mothers at home. She also became an interpreter for the larger railroad camp. The camp people simply turned to Teresa for her help, including the care of battered wives. Whenever Teresa engaged in any of this work, when possible, Luz accompanied her.

**I still do not know how it happened, but I think it was
the children of the mothers that brought us together.
Teachers would ask me to speak to the mothers
about a child, or children would need to be entered in
the school, or a child would be bad or not study
or would fight too much. Sometimes we could not understand
what we were saying to each other but our hands and movements.
Then sometimes mothers crying about things would**

**help, and we would all understand. Then sometimes the new
wives who had no children but expected a child would
ask for help, and I would look after her until our doctor
who visited our camp came and would tell me what to do.
And then sometimes married people would fight and
husbands would drink and hit their wives, and I had to
tell them to stop and to find out what was the problem.
It was good I was never hit, but it came close to that.
And sometimes it felt like I was still in the church house
where there was sometimes fighting and trouble. But
it felt good to be with the mothers and wives, my sisters.**

Little by little, Teresa—and Luz—even began to lead the women of the camp out into the larger city. She even took a few with her into the Loop. Teresa was by now well known and trusted by everyone in the camp. So when she and Francisco decided to buy a house on the east side of the city, the camp people protested and ultimately got a promise from Teresa that she would visit them regularly. She did from then on, for years.

Meanwhile the family prospered. The two girls and one of the boys went on to lead solid professional lives. Luz became a gifted art teacher, and her younger sister became a professional graphic designer. The younger son became an accountant. The older son, Juan, was seriously wounded in the Korean War and afterwards lived alone in a rural area some distance from Phoenix.

Over the years, Teresa and Pancho continued to live in the bungalow they had first purchased. And Pancho continued to work for the Pennsylvania Railroad.

Some years after working as a section foreman, he was offered a supervisory position that involved mostly deskwork. For a time, Pancho seriously considered taking the position then finally decided against it. As he told Teresa, he enjoyed working with his hands, and he enjoyed his old friends too much.

30

Francisco's Death

**Strange are the preparations
and arrangements to love
and to leave.**

Suddenly Francisco was dead. As the observer, I was unprepared for the event. Teresa was lost, suspended in shock as she first spoke of it. She received the news late one night after Pancho had gone off to work on a train wreck. He was crushed by a lifting crane that had slipped from its foundation.

Teresa spoke of his death long after the burial. For a long time afterwards, she said, daily tasks came slowly: preparing small foods, listening to her children and two grandchildren, going shopping. Her thoughts always wandered back to Francisco. The months following his death were the hardest; she often spoke to him directly as if he stood, sat, or lay with her.

**Had I known that you would die without me,
life broken in you,
I would have mourned you sooner.
I know now I loved you early, before marriage,
and now I come to love you more that you are gone from me.
Tears begin; moments of awareness touch remembrances
so deep. Slight memories return, images form,**

sounds mesh and living touch is here again.

Time waits outside itself;
we move softly with our past.

Days, weeks, months passed, and finally Teresa was speaking in her soft, gentle voice again. She believed it would be good for her to return to San Ignacio. There, she was told, she would begin to find an end to her pain.

She put her affairs in order in Chicago then asked her son Juan to take her to that mountain where she had first learned of Yomumuli and of the women of *Seataka*. In time, Juan took his mother to San Ignacio as she asked and waited for her. Later, at her insistence, he took her to his farm home near Phoenix. She had visited there before and said she wanted to stay. He made special room for her.

Before even leaving Chicago, Teresa had a dream of Francisco.

Smaller he curls awaiting burial,
a readying for the earth.
Railroad-hammered hands lie quiet,
less gnarled, less ready.
His face returns from layered-over pain
to childlike serenity, uncovered to a
gentler view.
Spent time draws up upon itself;
he sleeps less fitfully ...
draw slow the mourning curtain
keeps soft the gauze sounds of this room.

31

Teresa's Death

Teresa and I grew close over the course of my dreams. This is her story as told by me.

Years had passed. Teresa remained in her son's small farm and through dimming eyes, witnessed the growth of her children and the birth and growth of theirs. Friends of Juan's had come to know Teresa and slowly turned to her for counseling in crisis and grief. As in the railroad camp, she practiced loving each person she reached, and love returned to her just as when her children and grandchildren reached for her, and she easily embraced their needs.

Strange, how people in that area came to know of Teresa.
She always seemed a curious child herself,
holder of troubled children, soother of anger,
doer of things, a mender, a strengthener of affairs.
She traveled as she could, with and without Juan
and came to know much of that local farm world and its people.

Her son Juan was a product of her ways. He received small monetary help for his wartime scars and occasionally worked in nearby mines. Mostly, though, he chose to live a reclusive life, raising and bartering mules and horses for simple foodstuffs, implements, and basic necessities so as to live the simplest of lives. Thus Teresa fit in easily with her son's way of living.

Apart from their one trip to San Ignacio, Juan had not seen much of his mother for some time. He had not traveled to Chicago often except for the funeral of his father. After their trip to San Ignacio, he observed that his mother had aged considerably. She appeared older, spoke with a very gentle tone of voice, and her face had softened with deep lines. Still she stood tall in her small, rounded stature.

After his mother settled into his small adobe house, Juan recognized that she wished to have long solitary periods of meditation and silence and would speak only when she chose. He respected her wishes and fed and helped her as he could. Her life was now very small.

One night after Teresa had shared some stories about the church workhouse in Mexico, she asked that he listen, sounding as if her death was imminent.

**My special son ... I have wanted to be with you
because you are a man of strength and intuition and
your pain has made you gentle without anger.
You have witnessed the importance of loving and
the hurt that come from its absence. I sense that from
this experience has come your simple way of living
and love of all things and people. I have known that,
and now I need of your understanding.**

**I have come here to die. Dying, I believe,
will be the gentlest of moments I can have.
And being in this place of peace and speaking
with you of my journey, makes dying more of a dream
than I know that it is.**

**So listen, my son. Before I leave, you should know
that by a vision for me from Ometeotl, our creator,
he has instructed me to be a caretaker of the power of *Seataka*.
And he has asked that when I wish to die, I select a man
from among my children to hold this faith and power in trust.
I wondered why this was so, thinking *Seataka* were only women,**

and our creator knew my thoughts and responded.

He said he would have selected Luz if *Seataka*
were only women. Yet he selected a man to honor
men's returning role in loving and nurturing,
saying this will come to pass, begins now, and will be so
with men of feeling, intuition, and caring in their natures.
He said, I can select you, Juan, for this holding of power. In
nature, loving and nurturing, you are closest to *Seataka* in
being a man. And, among all my special children, you
are honored as a first part of man's returning role with
women in loving and nurturing.

So now accept this trust as you accept me. Hold
it in place. And in some moment, you will receive your own
words and vision from Ometeotl who will again place the
holding in a woman of *Seataka*. We cannot know when
that will be, of what race and age. But it will be a woman!

Come then, accept my trust my son,
And hold me as if I were a newborn child,
and nothing more need be said.

In the days that followed, Teresa appeared more childlike than her
son. The task of Ometeotl completed, she seemed fully free to spend
hours with ordinary things: watching stars, dawns, sunsets, peering into
the lives of small rodents, birds, and insects. Rabbits stopped to return
gazes. And the old woman spoke faintly from accumulated memories, at
times to herself and sometimes to the sky.

So long ago, I remember when winter senses and images
would first come to the camp. The high snow, unknown
beauty and bitterness. So long ago, the fingers
cold as ice in the silent winter.

And in Luz's school, a hand just touching my dark hair,
my neck glowing deep inside a brilliant orange yellow,
from the comfort felt from this teacher saying she
liked my long hair. She was tall, a beautiful woman,
helping us poor people with little money, saying to Juan,
"Here, try on this pair of shoes," and "You look so good."

I recall the strangeness I felt to accept charity,
which this woman turned into an exchange of love.
Sometime, when time will wait outside itself,
I will return to that past to be with that woman of love.

Teresa also recalled how life and death took place in old railroad boxcars, refashioned without wheels into homes. Bereft of means, tired looking, the cars were set down in the small railroad camp on the far east side of Chicago.

She found it likely that other Chicagoans were unaware of the tragedies and miracles happening in that place. They happened among the workaday poverty of new immigrants seeking prosperity in far North America. They came from many places to live between active railroad beds, busy with huge trains coming at all hours of the day and night. Their locomotives wheezed, churned their wheels, creaked, and drew long drawn-out whistles that altered dreams with deafening, comforting sounds. Harsh, plaintive wails and the clunking, swaying sounds of mutely following caravans of cars all had become indices of home. These memories mingled with the birth dates and death dates of the children of Ometeotl as they arrived summers and winters, a renewal of immigrants.

Into this midst, came a humane physician to care for the poor and alien in Teresa's small part of the world. Teresa gave birth and received death, assisted by this man. Later, as she learned his foreign ways of speaking and his mannerisms, they joined on births and deaths in those railroad cars. Teresa provided him with the needy to certify that life and death existed among the noises and networks of steel. When Teresa left, this old man, who was almost as old as Hernan had been and who was gruff in most ways, bent to hide his tears.

And slowly, Teresa was dying, using memories as prayer beads. She recalled family; her distant, imagined father; her wanted mother; Francisco; each child and their mannerisms known in special ways by a mother. She brought back each of the faces of undernourished children she had held in the workhouse. And always Teresa returned to Luz. "Luz, you count in small numbers to enlarge dreams. We have received love from you!"

Teresa imagined that she cradled all her children, all children. As she imagined this, sounds arose as small winds strung out, stretched past infinity and time beyond. A very slow time had arrived.

That one day, in early afternoon, the sun nearly overhead
and her important memories remembered, Teresa knelt to die.
She knelt for a time as if asleep and then slowly arose
to motion to each of seven directions. As she completed each
acknowledgement, she returned her hand to her head
then to seven parts of her skull.
She motioned to the north, the south, the east, the west,
to up, to down, and in the seventh motion
to the vertical center and direction of herself.

And then Teresa sat upon her earth and died alone,
surrounded by the world.

That evening Juan returned to find his mother sitting in her quiet death. He understood her wish, yet now he sat beside her and cried deeply. He cried, and he looked for her in the darkening desert evening and saw a huge rainbow in the setting sun. Even the mountains seemed in awe at the splendor of the banded lights cast out by Ometeotl. To the son, all seemed harmonized in a single vision. Birds and bushes, the cast of leaves, small animals, and the *cirio* settled in natural states to behold the moments of color and lights.

And when the sunset had dimmed and disappeared, the night resumed movement. Night passed moon and stars; time quickened the return to its natural pace. Night lasted, and day dawned a fresh color in shades of lavender and gold. The sun began its presence over Bacum, Leon, Kansas, Chicago, and finally reached over Teresa. And loving people awakened.

A physical Teresa died, yet Teresa's spirit as a
Woman of Power is always beginning and lives on.
That spirit infuses all women serving as bearers of goodness
and light in their walks of life … all women who
help men live whole in a new world. Amen.

CPSIA information can be obtained at www.ICGtesting.com
Printed in the USA
BVOW08s0659140915

417721BV00002B/240/P